I0762303

IN RUINS

DANIEL DAVIS WOOD

This edition published in Great Britain in 2021 by Splice,
54 George Street, Innerleithen EH44 6LJ.

Hardback Edition: ISBN 978-1-8380787-3-7
Paperback Edition: ISBN 978-1-8380787-4-4

IN RUINS

DANIEL DAVIS WOOD

SPLICE

I have words
That would be howled out in the desert air,
Where hearing should not latch them.

Shakespeare

From the base of the stairs rising up to the street, I could smell the sleet falling before I could see it. Some tension in the nighttime air, some tang of grit and masonry, called to mind cement and stone awash in sloppy wetness. I peered up into the stairwell, squinted through its lowlit haze, but all I could see of the world above was perfect, immaculate black. I felt myself pinned to the platform by the pack that bore down on my shoulders. I felt a creeping sultriness where the straps gathered clothes in my armpits. I felt my socks, soaked with sweat, stick to the soles of my feet, and I felt the dry heat of overnight travel trapped between my thighs. I stood dazed, I remember, hollowed out by far too many sleepless hours, until the choke of an overhead engine pulled me back to where I was. I saw my surroundings as if seeing anew and I saw where I needed to be. One hand reached for the railing and felt the sting of icy steel. The knuckles of the other rubbed at bloodshot eyes. Pitching against the midwinter air as a fresh blast bombarded the station, I stepped up to see if the city outside remained as I remembered it.

Memory lapses with distance and time. I'd boarded the train convinced I could see things as clearly as if I'd been gone just a day. All of a sudden, alone in the cold, I saw that I remembered details only vaguely. Street level brought me to a barren road and a view of terraces crammed together along the ridge of Castle Crag. Sleet that gushed through the beams of lights clouded the air with a tawny haze. From behind the bulk of the Balmoral, the North Bridge spanned the Waverley Valley to touch the easternmost edge of the Old Town. In the west, the floodlit cathedral and castle soared into the sky. Buildings had not relocated, of course, and footpaths had not changed directions, but absence, I realised, had dulled my recall of the substance and textures of things. All I'd preserved in my mind's eye were silhouettes of static structures, the contours of a cityscape bereft of anything sensuous. All I'd carried with me was a lifeless arrangement of outlines, a flat panorama of arcs and edges bolted into fixed positions. What returned to the city as I moved on foot was what my movement forced upon it.

Tenements slowly shifted with each onward step, jostling for space on the rise of rock like restless birds on a telegraph wire. Those lower down, close to the street, cleaved to the slope at the foot of the ridge while those above them dallied eastward down the spine. Bound for the hither edge of the gardens, headlong into the deluge of slush, I watched their striations, all straight lines and angles, bend and warp, ripple and sway. Windowsills and pediments that stood parallel to the street sliced into ducts and pipes that ran to rooftops and gutters. Scraps of sky spread out and shrank in gaps between gablets and chimneys. Sandstone façades stole spires from view, and wayward turrets set crowns upon buildings too dun, too squat, to justly wear them. A left hook onto Waverley Bridge. A swale of wind through the valley slapped me with a chill. I dipped down the decline alongside the gardens and watched the ridge ahead rise up, watched it gather the buildings together and drag them into the sky like a swell of sea dragging flotsam towards the crest of a wave. Another left hook at its pedestal routed me back to the station. A moment later, with a shuffle along the footbridge over the empty concourse, I found myself returning, returned, to the base of the stairs rising up to the street and the blackness of the world outside.

Memory lapses with distance and time. That was where and when those words spoke to me. I didn't know where I might go to get warm and wait for daybreak. That was when and why a piece of the past came back to me. Partway up to the road again, partway down to the platform, the staircase extends to a mezzanine where glass doors give onto a food court. Despite the locks and the shadows beyond the glass, there was no holding back the pulsing visions of what I knew lay inside. The twinkle of gilded tabletops, the bent legs of cheap aluminium stools. The sickening sweetness of frying oil, the floor smeared and spattered with grunge, and all of it embalmed in grim and flickering fluorescence. Often enough, too often perhaps, that hole had been a haven of mine, a space to sit out the cold and gather my thoughts and pull myself together. Standing there, though, I remembered a day when a cleaning woman, herself unclean, ambled over to where I sat and grunted out an eviction. Time to move on, lad, she said with a rasp that ripped me away from my words. I remember I gazed up at her not knowing at first what she wanted from me. I'd moved there from a seat on the concourse when the concourse became too cold. I couldn't see why I'd have to move again, much less why I'd been approached and asked to. I watched her squint at the looseleaf pages scattered over my table. Sprouts of stubble spotted a chin that lolled about on folds of fat. Foul brown stains begrimed her trousers; moisture at her throat had blemished her collar with streaks of grey. Only paying customers can use the facilities here, she said. Buy something first. Then you can sit.

She refused to listen when I told her I'd thrown out my coffee not even a minute ago. She refused to argue and simply said I couldn't stay seated unless I paid up. What made the encounter so galling for me, aside from having already bought myself the right to linger, was knowing she had no need to confront me to force me up and out. I'd been sitting there for hours, as I did so often then, and I'd just been preparing to leave when the cleaner chose to approach. What made the encounter so galling was the itch of its indignity, the grating fact of being forced to sit there, to sit beneath her, and to bear humiliation at the behest of a person so pathetic. As suddenly as I felt incensed by her presence beside me, I also felt certain that she'd been watching her prey from afar for a while. She'd begun plotting against me long before she spoke, but she'd bided her time and awaited a false move that would give her cause to strike. The very act of walking to me and ordering me to rise from my seat swelled our exchange about rules and procedures out of all proportion to the venue and the offence. My misdemeanour was breathtakingly petty. It didn't warrant the energy she expended on resolving it, it didn't deserve the consideration she compelled me to give it, and as thoughts of this sort besieged me in the heat of that eternal moment, I felt brewing in me a resentment no less outsized for the encounter. An inner blaze reddened my face as I rose from my seat to push past her, to wade through the ecstatic glory of her conqueror's aura, but until I returned to those stairs in search of shelter from the sleet, I'm sure my thoughts hadn't dwelt on her since the day we'd clashed. I stared at the lock on the doors, the chinks of chain coiled over the handles, and I wondered then, as I wonder still, if that clash did not birth the sense of pursuit that has dogged me for so long I can't properly measure the time. All I want, all I hope I might find, is a place to sit still and stay quiet awhile, but more and more often these days I'm certain I'll always be a hunted man.

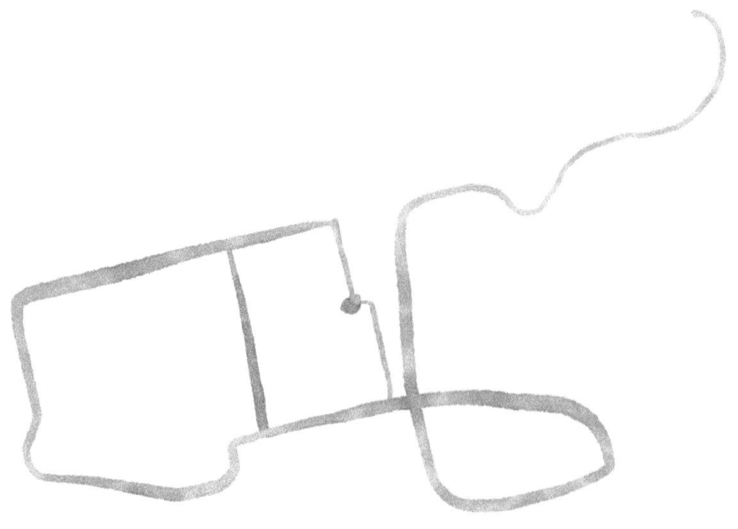

Dawn broke grey overhead. Red lights brought a bus to a halt. A nearby taxi, parked at the curb, let its service sign glow although the engine made no sound. The driver I glimpsed through the sleet-spattered window sat asleep in his seat, cramped up with his knees against the steering wheel and both arms curled round his thighs. But I never would've hailed him even if I'd wanted to. I turned aside and set off again in the direction of the gardens. This time I walked on without veering off-course, tracking the length of the wrought iron fence, to pass the almighty black pike that shelters the whitewashed form of Walter Scott. Where the fence arrives at a corner, slippery stones lead to the stairs that ascend the slope of the Mound. Climbing those stairs called up the first time, as well as the last, that everything I could see then had passed before my eyes.

Day of arrival, years ago. Morning advanced with a light that made the cloudless sky an almost violent blue. A different path that day, uphill and then down again, rambling through the closes and wynds that gouge passageways between the buildings of the Old Town. Just to walk the streets, I remember, was to experience something elemental. The shadowed sides of gorges of stone gave a chill to the touch. In thickets of lichen and moss, extrusions of dew glistened and ran rivulets into the gutters. The silver expanse of the Firth of Forth glimmered beyond the steeple of the Tron. Seagulls wheeled overhead and yowled laments through empty streets. I thought I could name what I felt at that moment almost as soon as it woke inside me. This place felt like mine. What I'd said to the people I left behind when I went abroad to put down new roots was that I'd finally found a place I felt I could make my home. Later, though, I realised I'd said it back-to-front. What I'd really felt was that I'd somehow found my way to a home I'd never seen before. What I'd found was a place I felt had been awaiting me, as if I shared a spirit with it and I'd spent my life unknowingly seeking it out. What was in reality an arrival felt to me like a return.

Day of departure, years after that. No less bright and brilliant, although a harsher, longer winter had buried the green of the gardens beneath tattered leaves and pools of sludge. I was moving fast to make my train, dashing down the stairs at the Mound, when I saw Celeste on the uphill footpath. I saw she'd seen me, too. She wore a rainbow sarong around her waist and a svelte blue coat that clung to the curves of her body. For a moment she robbed me of breath and thought. Beside her walked another woman, her sister visiting for the weekend, and as I descended the stairs while the two of them climbed the bend in the road, I threw Celeste a smile which I hoped would catch her eye so that we might stop and speak one last time before I left for good. But even though I saw her see me, she didn't stop moving and didn't slow down. In fact she turned aside and made to appear as if she didn't know me at all. She laughed at something her sister said, a little too theatrically, and as they walked past she adjusted the orange headscarf she'd taken to wearing and then groped about in her bag in search of cigarettes. Half an hour earlier, before I scribbled a farewell note to Hannah, I'd left my keys on the kitchen table and pulled the front door closed. Celeste hadn't been there when I walked out and her absence had disturbed me. I worried that it held some secret meaning beyond my ken. Then all of a sudden she was there in my face, right there by those stairs, and whatever mysteries she raised with her absence were overshadowed by those she raised with the ignorance she feigned when all I wished for her to do was stop so I could say goodbye.

In rainfall that softened and started to hiss as it dwindled into a drizzle, I curved along the Mound and climbed to Castle Crag. On the far side of the street, a skip overflowed with trash. Beside it a brawl of blankets and cardboard shifted and hacked out a cough. Onward momentum, a jolt up the incline. As I strained to move I wondered whether I'd ever met whoever took refuge in all that rubbish. Often those skips had waymarked the route I'd take home after work each day my first winter. I couldn't set out until dark, nearer to midnight than dusk, and every time I'd suffer a chill more spiteful than any I'd felt before. Afternoons at the café meant hours of ladling broth. The broth was warm and nourishing, but never so popular that I could sell out as much as I brewed each day. Stefan told me I should just dump whatever hadn't moved by closing time. The slop was useless waste, he said. It'd go rancid overnight. Best to bin it and head on home. But as soon as I heard those words I knew I couldn't follow his orders, and so every night in secret I'd split the leftover broth between a dozen disposable bowls and I'd take them onto the streets. From South Bridge down to Rose Street, then via the Mound to the Grassmarket. Concrete and flagstone slicked with ice. Out to Tollcross and Bruntsfield before heading home through the Meadows. Crunch of frost on crisp grass. Without a word I'd place each bowl at the feet of the beggars I passed on my way. There but for the grace of God go I, I always thought. Every night, night after night. That's a thought I know I'll take with me to the grave.

The blankets and cardboard coughed again.

An empty bus trundled up the street.

At a plod I struggled towards the Royal Mile. I pulled at the straps on my shoulders to shift some weight onto my back.

Sometime during the night, during a break in the falling sleet, some drunkard had dropped a hat on the head of David Hume. As the great man sat in solemnity on the edge of the Lawnmarket, a horrid orange traffic cone adorned him like a dunce's cap.

A black cab rushed past from someplace behind me. Suddenly it turned and bustled downhill over broken road. Hazed by its rising exhaust, far out over the firth, dawn was slowly bleaching grey sky into white. The struggling sun, dampened by fog, cast wan light into mist. Seagulls excited by daybreak drew curvatures across the horizon. This time, though, on this day of return, they swerved and swooped without a sound.

There's a kink in the road at Greyfriars Kirkyard. That's what I had to reach. It would set me off through the Meadows towards Marchmont on the far side. Instead, though, I reached out to touch the plinth, braced myself with a hand on one corner, and leant against it and spent a long time just looking into space ahead of me. All I had to do, I knew, was walk the mile between where I stood and where I needed to put myself. All I had to do was take a step forward, and then another, and go and get there and knock on the door. But the day was still too young, too dark, for anyone to be awake. But dampness stank my clothes and wet hair clung to my brow, and this was no state in which to show up unannounced. But I didn't even know exactly where I wanted to be, or which of the houses I intended to plead for respite in. At a loss I relinquished my will to the ways of the world around me. I stepped back and let the world lead me where it would; I gave in and let my surroundings suggest what I should do.

I'd hated that statue of Hume from the moment I set eyes on it. Because I respect and revere the man himself, I hate the way the statue makes him look ridiculous. His glorious iconoclasm had been one of the forces that drew me towards those hallowed streets in the first place. His spite for sophistry and superstition had roused in me a love of the climate in which he'd flaunted his ferocious intellect. But he wasn't exactly what you'd call a handsome fellow. He had googly eyes and a triple chin and the flabbiness around his gut sagged almost to his toes. You'd never want to see a man like Hume less than fully clothed. Despite all that, his sadistic sculptor had draped him in a toga and set him reclining with one breast exposed to the air. The orange cone on his head clashed with the jade of faded bronze, I thought, but whoever had used it to make jest of Hume had only finished the job his sculptor had begun. His eyes seemed sullen behind the water that dribbled off the brim of his hat. Who could begrudge him his sorrow?

Distant daylight stained the sky through gaps between the clouds over Fife. I turned to the staircase behind the bank that towered over Hume. My wet feet slipped around in shoes gone damp from the uppers to the soles. Spittle, lit up by dawn, swirled like a storm of midges through the tranche of open air between the Mound and Calton

Hill. Marchmont lay in the other direction. So did whatever future I might hope to make.

I hobbled down the stairs and tumbled out at the southernmost reach of Waverley Bridge.

Passing alongside the station this time, I twisted a path towards the World's End and crossed the traces of gold on the ground that ghost the site of the Flodden Wall. A host of memories slumbered there. No way to move fast enough to escape them all. I shot uphill towards the Tron and watched another empty bus chug northward over North Bridge. It cut its lights at my corner. I crossed the bridge in its wake and stepped into a fossilised day on that very spot on my first weekend in the city. Police had kept the bridge cordoned off. A man of dubious sanity had perched himself on a ledge that jutted out over train tracks. I'd seen him on the Saturday morning. He sat on the ledge like a child on a pier, swinging his legs in the air. Officers in uniform crowded together beneath him. All of them looked straight up at him and one blurted something unintelligible into a hissing megaphone. The bridge remained closed until Sunday after dark. Rumours raced through the streets in the meantime. People said he was a family man. They said he'd lost a lifelong job too suddenly to support his dependents anymore. A spectacular sun shone down all weekend, bathing the city in the sort of warmth that feels like a miracle at the fag end of winter, but none of it made any difference to the wreck on the ledge. He suffered so intensely, was so profoundly dislocated from the glory of his surroundings, that he could see no path forward but the one beneath his feet, the rails of steel that would bring his life to an end.

No man ever threw away life while it was worth keeping. That's what Hume had to say on the subject, and his words returned to me on that site exactly as they'd come to me when I heard, later on, what had happened there. The man on the ledge had been cursed with such incurable depravity, or gloominess of temper, that it poisoned all his enjoyment and rendered him equally miserable as if he had been loaded with the most grievous misfortunes. He wouldn't be talked out of making the leap. He couldn't be apprehended before he'd launched himself into the air. He also wasn't the only man to drop off that ledge during my time in the city; I can remember at least half-a-dozen others. Even so, he stands out to me for having been the first to take his life before someone else had the chance to take control of it from him.

Chains still fastened the gates outside the philosopher's tomb. A sign beside them said the cemetery would be open at sunrise. Maybe some groundskeeper put it there as a joke. Dawn had arrived but the sun remained hidden and that might have been reason enough to keep the place locked up. Through the black bars of the gates I caught a glimpse of a sleeping bag. Faded green, sheathed in a patina of rime. With a rustle it shifted against a headstone. Hume had been laid to rest nearby, on a spot now marked by a monstrous cylinder of stone, a gargantuan eyesore girdled with gravel and garbage. Unable to enter and see it again, I crossed the road and urged my feet up Calton Hill to honour Hume in a different way.

Cold morning air reached into my throat and ripped out breaths that burst into vapour. The bole of Arthur's Seat in the south emerged above the crags that encircled the mountain, crags like solid rings of rock in orbit around some planetary goliath. The path that passes by Nelson's Column, alongside the Parthenon replica left in a half-finished state, led me to a brambled cliff commanding a view of the New Town. That was, I knew, where Hume had gone each day on his morning constitutional. Even in the piss and smirr, it wasn't hard to see why. The surface of the Firth of Forth caught a daub of sunlight and smudged it to the coast of Fife, and the fringes of the city crept out towards the edge of the water. In the space between my rocky ledge and the waves that licked at the land, the streets convulsed with smokestacks and spires, tenements, gasworks, stadiums, churches and terraces and shuttered shops. Block after block of sandstone structures glowed with the caramel glaze of streetlights on low. They crowded in close along roads that refused to waver, roads that gave this half of the city the sharp and pointed precision so foreign to the other. Suddenly the sun arrived in beams that broke through the grey to play across the silvering sea. All at once the streetlights went dark and sucked the last traces of warmth from the city, and then, not too far away, rhythmic footsteps crunching stones grew louder as they drew near to me.

Stepping back from the ledge, across a mound of heather, I fell onto a cold wet bench as the jogger muddled by. Bald and old, blanched red with exertion, he wore shorts and a singlet and moved with dolly steps. After he'd passed, my backpack slipped off to thud onto the dirt and grass. In its absence I felt I'd grown a pair of wings and begun to fly. I leant back and looked out at the sprawl of the city. Hume, I imagined, would have taken his leisure in much the same spot on some idle summer's day and, like me, would've watched the passersby of so many centuries ago. Then again, he could afford to indulge in things like that. Sit down and ruminate at leisure. Write a few learned treatises on the vagaries of human existence. He'd enjoyed a sensational family fortune. He'd been free to not devote his idle moments to the endless task of buying himself one more weary day of life.

I drew a deep breath and let my eyes drop, let them close. If not for the cold I might have fallen asleep right there on that bench. Everything smelled fine and fresh, washed newly clean by the sleet. I opened my eyes and watched the sun return a shine to the New Town. Then I opened my backpack for paper and pen to make note of all the details that had sprung to mind so far. Too early, still, to strike out for Marchmont, wherever I finally decided to go, but I had to pass the morning one way or another. I started unthreading thoughts and memories from the solid structures I'd woven them into. I tried to find ways of twisting them into a tapestry of words.

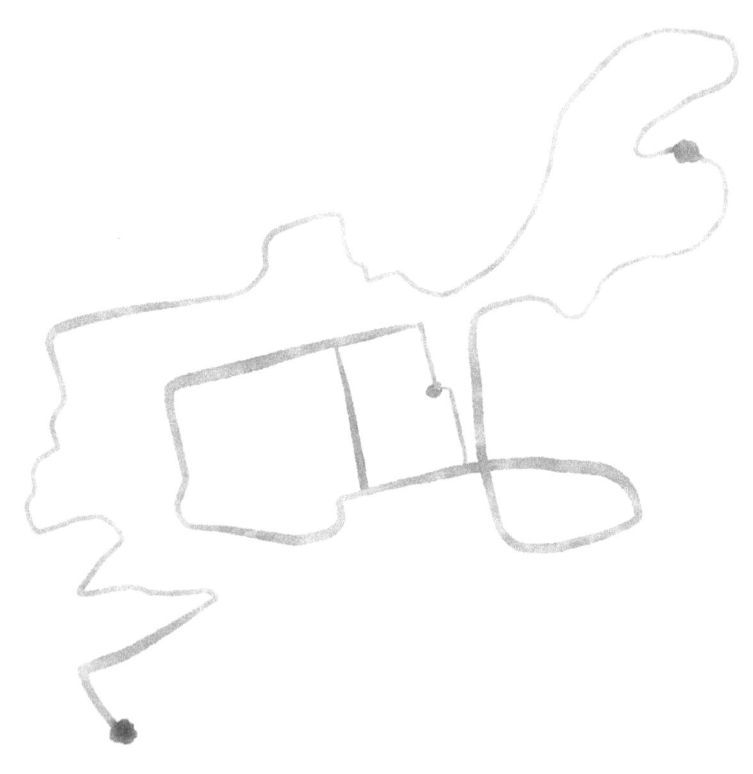

Steam unfurled from the cup beside me and gave rise to the stink of burnt coffee. So what if it was rank? All I hoped to do just then was sit at the window and savour the smell. Through the fogging glass I watched the Grassmarket grind into life. At the base of Granny's Green, two thin guys on pedal taxis set up their kit for the day ahead. Could I rest my forehead against the pane and sleep and wake and find the coffee still warm? Then wrap my hands around the cup and take a sip and return it to where it remained, untouched, and close my eyes again? I knew I couldn't. I had to sit awake to prolong my time indoors. I had to sit and write to keep myself from falling asleep. Writing, working, forward momentum, would earn me permission to linger awhile. Aimlessness at the window would mean a quick drink and an early departure.

I tilted forward and squinted to peer down the street to the door of Niall's old shop. He'd spent his weekends in there selling vintage clothes on behalf of the bosses he called the Midlothian Mafia. Until I found my seat at that window, I'd been thinking he still worked there. Maybe, I thought, I'd find him lounging about at his counter instead of swinging open his door to answer a knock he wouldn't expect. But the pedal taxis set my memory to rights. The dun brick walls of the castle towered above where the two men fastened carriages to their bikes. Watching them there and thinking on Niall, I felt I'd been suddenly swept along by the invisible ways of the world, as if the flow of the morning had guided me to that spot.

Life underway at dawn had led me down from Calton Hill and into the streets below. Blackbirds, thrush, and meadowlarks dashed from bush to bush on either side of the footpath I descended. Flowers cowered into buds, bracing against the turn of the season, and rocks overgrown with grass were clawed from below by gorse. Another jogger sprung into view at the base of the path and staggered uphill as I passed him to reach the road. Buses and cabs, a few early cars. Leafless trees, skeletons of sycamores, and soot-stained houses with windows lit up only at the edges of thick cotton curtains. Rising winds skipped plastic bags and bottles across the pavements. Blindly I wandered the warren of backstreets around the archives. At last I emerged into St. Andrew Square with a cold blast roaring up from the harbour. Ducking to shield myself from the onslaught of the cold, I darted towards the sheltered calm of Rose Street and that was where I found myself abruptly facing Andrej.

I recognised him and I knew that I knew him before I was able to conjure his name. In the heartbeat between the moment of recognition and my remembrance of him, I was struck by the anxious thought that he might see me and place me first and approach me as someone familiar.

He stood at the mouth of the road and hunched as he flicked through a bundle of papers. Then he looked up and revealed to me the features I knew well. Narrowed eyes, a harried brow, as of a man exerting himself to pick out the fine print on a paper too far away to read. A big, bulbous nose, purpled by broken capillaries, and a spray of grey across his chin. Plain black shoes and black trousers worn with a belt, a white collared shirt tucked in tight, and a dark brown corduroy blazer, unbuttoned, drooping around his cadaverous frame.

The blazer, I saw, was exactly the one he'd been wearing the day we met at the World's End. Springtime had started to sweeten the air of the city. Everyone else, including me, had taken to wearing shirts or singlets and slacks or shorts and a pair of jandals. Andrej prowled around us with the look of a character from a period film, silent and almost sepia toned, as if he'd stepped off a steam engine from far beyond the Iron Curtain at about the time that Khrushchev was flexing his muscles. He'd walked through the door in that suit and clutched a briefcase of smooth brown leather and mumbled a formal greeting in an accent we learnt was Hungarian. Over the following weeks he spoke of little else besides his mission, his determination, to earn enough money to pay his way and send the remainder back to his mother in some nameless village on the *puszta*. He took up selling *The Big Issue* to passersby on Princes Street. I guess he never made enough to make his way home to his mother again. More than a decade later, around the corner from where he used to stand, he nestled a stack of magazines into the crook of his arm and with his free hand he offered a single copy to me.

Big Issue, he said. More a statement than a question. He awaited a response. I found I couldn't move. I searched his empty eyes for some sign that he knew who I was. According to rumours I remembered, he'd sold heroin as well as magazines. If there was any truth to the gossip, I'm sure he never took drugs himself. He had only one source of pleasure. He gave his chess set more space in that briefcase than what he kept reserved for clothes. He'd conquered me in a matter of minutes the first and only time we contended. Later on, a Ukrainian vagrant had arrived at the World's End to stay with a friend for a few weeks and Andrej had latched onto him as a worthier opponent. The two of them played for hours at a time, long into the night, and more often than not I'd find them still playing, each man grumbling beneath his breath, when I rose to get ready for work in the morning.

Yes? he said. *Big Issue.*

The magazine hovered between us.

With thoughts elsewhere I reached into a pocket and fumbled for some coins. Only when my fingers jangled them did I remember I had nothing to spare. I thought of the coffee I knew I'd need, the coffee that would buy me warmth and shelter, and I turned Andrej down with a brusque apology although I couldn't turn away. I peered into his eyes. Did any lasting memory of me linger beyond their surfaces? Not as far as I could tell. Somewhere inside myself, I think, I'd supposed that my return, unannounced, might've somehow ruptured the lives of the people I'd once known, the people who'd remained in my absence. Yet coming so close to Andrej, struck dumb like some bewildered beast, I felt these thoughts collapse and implode. Remembering nothing of who I was, and having undergone no changes of his own, he made me feel as if I'd never been there before, as if the life I used to live simply never existed, as if my movements through the world were of no consequence to others at all. Invisible to anyone I might encounter now, untethered to any aspect of my new surroundings, I felt liberated and powerless, free and condemned to be free, released by fate to float through the city as if I'd become nothing more than a boundless, bodiless breeze.

Andrej stepped to the side and gestured into Rose Street, like an usher in a theatre showing the way to the stalls. His movements released me from the spell I'd cast on myself. I turned my eyes to the ground and stepped around him and set off slowly across the stones.

A few more seagulls squabbled overhead, flailing about in a fight over scraps. A rat beside an overflowing bin gorged itself on a hunk of fish that someone had dropped on the pavement. At Hanover Street a man and a dog slept together beneath a tattered blanket. The wind had turned the man's lips mauve. The dog awoke and cocked an eye as I prepared to cross the road. Back when I'd made my rounds that winter, that corner had been on my nightly route and perhaps that man had been there too. There but for the grace of God go I. I couldn't stop the thought from coming back to me there, even though all the graces I'd received in the meantime seemed to have run their distance. There but for the sympathy of those I used to know. If, I thought, they cared enough to know me anymore.

I remembered one night when one man asked me if I'd literally give him the shirt off my back. He'd approached me after I'd served a bowl of soup to another man. If he'd seen me hand it over, as I'm sure he did, he'd kept his distance until I'd moved on and then he sprinted to catch up to me. He apologised for his appearance, breathless and beaded with sweat, before asking politely if he might make an odd request. I worried for a moment that he'd proposition me. Instead he told me a lie that stunned me with its audacity. I'm not from around here, he said with an unmistakable Lothian accent. I just arrived, just got off the bus, and none of the shops are open this late but, you see, I've got two young kids, nine and seven, who live here with their mother, and I'm supposed to go see them tomorrow and I need to make a good impression.

He held out his hands, palms upturned, in a shrug of helplessness. I meant to buy a new shirt, he said, so I don't look so shabby when I pick them up, but now, you see, I don't have the chance to find a shop. He'd recently shaved but his teeth were yellow and the stale reek of homelessness hung about his clothes. As he went on he saturated his story with so much manufactured earnestness, so much confected sincerity, that I felt shame on his behalf, I felt ashamed to let him speak on, I felt ashamed to entertain him by standing and listening to more of his story. What I'm asking, he said, is if you might be able to help me out with a shirt.

I didn't say yes, I didn't say no. I didn't say anything at all. I felt so ashamed for the man that I couldn't bring myself to speak. I unzipped my hoodie in the middle of the street, in the middle of the night, and slipped it off to slip out of my shirt. Winter snapped at my back and chest and all the skin I exposed to its bite. After the shirt exchanged hands I hurried back into my hoodie and then, without a word, I watched the man burst into tears and lift the shirt to his face to crumple it into his eyes. I halted before him, unsure of how to conduct myself, while he clutched at the shirt and scrunched it against his forehead and heaved deep sobs of distress and burbled, Thank you— Thank you— and remained like that, blubbering thanks, as I nodded to him and edged away and started off for home. I couldn't look at Hanover Street and not see the haggard form of the man rise up from the asphalt like a spectre from a grave. Was he still out on the streets somewhere? Did he still wear my clothes? Might he be carrying with him some small memory of me?

At work the following day I'd told Sandy about what had happened. Then, at his urging, I told him what I'd done to attract attention. A short and pudgy troll who reeked of rolled tobacco, Sandy was a tetchy old pessimist who began every sentence with a groan. He sported a mad scientist's frazzled hair and bottle lens bifocals, and he cultivated a handlebar moustache to cover up his dangling jowls. Given the politics he wore on his sleeve, I'd assumed my nighttime goodwill would draw from him at least a grunt of solidarity. He was a decade past retirement age, but, a few years beforehand, a rotten employer had swindled him out of a liveable pension. Now, to supplement his anaemic income, he'd been forced to find work at the café, and this had committed him so staunchly to the cause of contemporary communism that he often served the customers propaganda with their coffees. Far from what I'd expected, though, he only warned me not to let Stefan know what I'd been doing, and when I arrived at work the next morning I found that he'd halved the daily output of winter broth. The broth sold out every day after that. My nightly rounds came abruptly to an end. After sundown, all across the city, a dozen empty stomachs went unfilled, a dozen freezing bodies went unwarmed.

Only when I came to Frederick Street did I realise that Sandy must have foreseen what would happen to the café and was doing what he could to fend it off. Where had he ended up? Council housing, probably. Possibly even the streets. The café closed down the following summer. Property damage put it on edge and then the health inspectors discovered traces of rats in the last place you'd want rats to be. The cost of repairs was already high and the fine on top of that was too steep for Stefan to keep things afloat.

The attack had occurred just as I finished my shift one night at the height of summer. Two girls walked in with two bottles of vodka and locked themselves in the bathroom. I thumped on the door and ordered them out, told them I had to lock up. I listened to their giggles and gulps and understood they wouldn't leave. I went to find the key to the lock but the front door banged open, kicked in, and bent to one side on buckling hinges, and over the threshold lunged a livid guy, a guy my age, about my size, screaming, enraged, shirtless and cut, covered in tattoos and howling at me for having abused his darlings. The bathroom latch switched open. The girls eased through the door. They tottered out with an empty bottle and the mobile phone they'd used to call for the screamer. He seized me by the collar, yanked me close to snarl in my face, then he unleashed a whiplike jab and I felt my cheekbone crack. Blood beat fierce heat into my head. The screamer hurled me onto the ground. I scrambled to support myself at the edge of the service counter, hoping to grip onto it and rise to my feet again, but then, within reach of where he stood, I spotted the blade I'd been using to slice up sandwiches all day.

I'm ashamed to say now that my first instinct was to protect the cash in the till. Even at risk of injury, even at risk of death, reflex moved me to defend the day's takings instead of simply bolting. I leapt for the knife while the screamer reached for a nearby chair. My fingers had barely brushed the handle before the chair came crashing down. It smashed into my back and my shoulder, smashed me onto the floor, smashed against the countertop, splintered into shards. The screamer, still screaming, gripped a stake that used to be a leg of the chair and took it outside to shatter the windows, one at a time, in piercing, percussive explosions of glass. I didn't know exactly when the two girls had left the building, but as soon as I saw the screamer outside I shuttered the windows and locked the door and stood there, bruised and bloodied, broken-boned, choking on my gasps and listening to the alarm that bleated above the screamer's blows. At some stage I know I called the police, although I don't remember it. All I remember next is calling Stefan to tell him what had happened. I remember giving him my assurance that all the money, his money, was safe. He said he was sorry for what I'd suffered and promised to pay me a bonus. The promise was without substance, of course, and no bonus, nothing but trouble, ever came to me.

The very next day was the day the inspectors discovered the rats. The authorities came to check up on the aftermath of the vandalism. What they found were pellets of poo in a tray of millionaire's shortbread. We were given a week to get rid of the problem but we weren't allowed to bait with poison. Sandy bought some sticky paper. It lay on the floor for a couple of days with cake crumbs sprinkled in the middle. When I showed up for a morning shift, four or five days after the assault, I found, affixed to the trap, a bundle of marmalade fur. It peered up at me, helplessly, through black eyes that glistened with what seemed almost like tears. Fully one side of its body was glued to the adhesive surface but the goddamn creature hadn't even shown enough decency to give up and die. It trembled, meek and supplicant, as I loomed over it and looked down. It scratched at the floor with one loose leg in a vain attempt to scurry away. I plucked it off the ground by the corner of the paper and took the screeching thing to the Meadows. I couldn't kill it. I didn't know how. The best I could do was set it free. I had to use a pencil to pry it loose. I shoved the pencil beneath its ribcage and tried to wiggle the animal off. I peeled it from the paper with an awful shredding sound, like fabric ripped on a nail. The rat leapt onto the grass and scampered away, raw and almost hairless on one whole side of its body. Clumps of ginger, clotted with blood, still stuck to the flimsy trap. That's to say nothing of the stench. I dry-heaved and swilled up a mouthful of saliva to spit out my disgust. When I returned to the café, I called Sandy and told him I refused to do anything like that ever again. He said we were fighting a losing battle anyway. Over the previous few days, he told me, he'd found enough droppings to fill a cappuccino mug. Catching a single rat meant nothing in the face of a full-scale infestation.

I ended up jumping ship early on. The business went under a couple months later. At a certain point my pay was two weeks overdue and I'd started working for IOUs that I knew would never be honoured. To my own surprise I realised I had too much self-respect to keep on swallowing the bullshit promises Stefan tried to feed me. I refused to incur the indignity of being dismissed from the drudgery of the minimum wage in a gig only one step up from stacking shelves at Sainsbury's. But did my abrupt departure hasten the closure of the café and the termination of the job that put a roof over Sandy's head? If Sandy slept on the streets these days, how much of his destitution had been brought about by me?

On Frederick Street a shabby terrace still housed the first place I'd found any work. A garish greasy spoon. An all-day breakfast den. It left me broke and broken-hearted.

I couldn't even look up from the footpath as I sauntered past its doors. I'd hated the place so intensely that within a week of arriving there I'd started to fuck with the food. I'd drop a gob of spit into the depths of a prawn cocktail. I'd season a bowl of scrambled eggs with detritus I plucked from my nose. These were my small thrashings, my attempts at subterfuge, against the iron grip of the tyrant who oppressed the place. She'd fled the regime in Moldova when she was only a teenage girl. Now she ruled over a dozen underlings who'd come to Britain from Poland or the Czech Republic or one of the other satellite states of the crumbled USSR. She employed them, and employed me, at an hourly rate far less than the minimum wage, then at the end of the day she'd pool together everyone's tips and use our personal takings to top up our pay so that we received the minimum thanks to our own so-called contributions. Naturally the remaining cash found its way into her purse, and, while she sat down to count what we'd collected, we always had to endure a lecture that rubbed salt in the wound.

She told us all about communism and its evils. She recalled how painful it had been for her to put in a day's work in Chișinău and know that the fruits of her labours wouldn't be hers alone to enjoy. She articulated her grievances without a hint of irony. Once, I remember, she lamented that when she'd started waiting tables at thirteen years of age, she'd spent so many hours on her feet that her shoes fell apart and she had so few earnings to show for it that she couldn't purchase new ones. She told me this as I prepared to walk home on blistered heels tortured by the ragged insoles of shoes I couldn't replace. Maybe I should've told her that, but I didn't want to argue. She would've leapt at the chance to reel off the appalling abstractions I couldn't possibly fathom, the restrictions on free expression, the terror of the secret police, and anyway I knew I'd suffer her wrath for having the gall to speak up. Her name was Alla, fittingly enough, and her rages against the beleaguered staff provoked a babble like that of terrified Muslims suffering torment from above.

That said, she paid me my due, which is more than Stefan ever did. When the café went into liquidation, I pressed him for what he owed me. When he refused to hand it over, I shot for legal recompense. A tribunal was arranged. He didn't show up for the hearing. I won by default, but winning turned out to be useless. I never got what was mine and he got away without setting things right. Halfway through the following winter I spotted him on the Causewayside. His style was so unmistakable that I recognised him from behind. A ponytail fell past his shoulders, streaked with silver and grey, and he'd dressed himself at odds with the demands of the season. He wore shorts that didn't reach his knees and socks pulled up high to cover his calves. He stopped at the edge of moving traffic to wait for a chance to cross the road. I had nothing left to lose, so I thought I'd pursue my complaint. I walked up to him and stood beside him and waited to see if he'd notice me. Slowly he turned his head, slowly his eyes met mine. What did he see when he looked at me? I wanted only to destroy him, to ruin him, to rip him into bloodied pieces, to seize him by the throat and smash his face against a pole, and my gaze must have shot out some sense of fury because before I said a word he bolted onto the bitumen, straight into the oncoming cars. Horns began to blare and shouts exploded from windows while he ducked and dashed between bumpers and fenders until he reached the far side of the street.

All I could do, as traffic tore past, was stand there dumbstruck, in total disbelief. What made the experience so strange wasn't just that he'd done it. What made it so strange was that I'd once done much the same when someone demanded money from me. Where Abbeymount severs Croft-an-Righ from the lower end of Regent Road Park, a railway overpass stretches shadows across a section of the street. I'd been walking through there near dark one night when a gang of four men emerged and stopped me in my tracks. One man grabbed at the scarf around my throat and threw me up against the overpass pillar. The others circled around me like wolves and instantly I saw the scale of my sheer, unforgivable stupidity. Stefan only ever paid his staff in cash, two weeks in arrears each time. Because I'd been paid the previous day, my wallet was fat with a fortnight's earnings. To be injured, wounded, would've been more dignified than to live with the loss of what I'd worked so hard for. I decided as much on the spot. I'd been robbed once already that year and I refused to muddle through the degradation again. The leader of the pack barked in my face. He ordered me to hand over whatever I was carrying. I feigned misunderstanding, pretended I couldn't converse in English, and managed to stall long enough to leave him taken aback. In his moment of hesitation I heard the growl of approaching cars and I reached up to my scarf, wrapped my hands around his fists, clutched at him where he held onto me, and dragged him with me into the street, straight into the path of the traffic. On reflex he released me, even shoved me away from him, and when I recovered from the jolt I vaulted the gates to the park and raced uphill. I turned back only briefly to glimpse him watching me the way I suppose I'd watched Stefan when he scampered off.

Now a gap opened up in the rush of morning buses. A glimpse of the Princes Street Gardens on the far side of the traffic. Beneath the commanding view of the castle, people filtered onto the footpaths. Early risers strode along while hungover vagrants stumbled out of wherever they'd braved the night. I braced against the wind and slipped through the gate at the feet of the mounted dragoon. I took the gardens all to myself and called up traces of their stories. Mornings spent scribbling names and dates in my own little book of the dead. St. Cuthbert's nestles behind a spiked iron gate, crowded in by headstones blackened by soot and rot. In that or another burial ground, Calton Hill or Greyfriars, my notebook collected copies of epitaphs etched in granite. The point wasn't really to keep a private record of facts. The point was simply to write, to feel something flow onto the page. To capture the most ephemeral residue of stories told in secret, or else in need of telling, and to sketch out a map of those spaces beyond which stories welled unseen, spaces beneath the skin of a city where stories seethe.

These days, of course, nothing remains of the scraps of events I gleaned from those graveyards. All that remains is what I learnt of what lies underfoot. Beneath the jagged blackstone at the base of Castle Crag, a path descends the slope to the gardens and dives into the vacant air of what was once a stagnant loch. The stench of the cesspit used to extend for miles around. All sorts of waste polluted the waters. Broken belongings, rotten food, animals dead and decaying. Human shit dumped on the High Street would dribble downhill to splosh into the mess. People were thrown in as well. Thieves and whores and witches. They'd have their thumbs nailed into their kneecaps before a crowd that had gathered high upon the crag would hurl them into the loch. A crust grew over the water. Sunbaked faeces and bile and, in winter, ice. How would a human body break against that septic surface? Bones would shatter and skin would split, spilling out flesh and entrails. To condemn a person to that sort of death was clearly to rob them of something more than life.

Thoughts like these bombarded me as I made my ascent. So did fine fresh rain. Wet grass splotched over with rotten leaves. Barren branches clawed upward, out of the muddied hillside. These were the sights that used to release the stories from where they inhered in the stones. They were sights that I knew could calm the endless murmur in my head, could focus it and refine it and give it a purity it lacked when not engaged in storytelling. Maybe that makes the stories a cheat. Often I'd turn my thoughts to them as a way of honouring the invisible elements of the world I was passing through. It's equally possible that they were my way of opting out of the world altogether. You could say I sustained an intellectual engagement with the history of a place. You could also say I liked to con myself into deferring the need to engage with what was right before my eyes.

Castle Terrace offered a haven from the city as the streets began to heave. The lowing of distant horns, a siren, the chirp of bells on bikes, but nobody, nobody, near the castle except for the soldiers who guarded the drawbridge. Were they the same two men I'd seen on my last night inside those walls? After a month of slaving under the dictatorship of Alla, the castle, too, had given me refuge. There I'd found a new job, still dishing food, still paid only a pittance, but mercifully a world away from the grease of Frederick Street. Not that there was nothing to complain about. Too often the patrons were English toffs hosting weddings for their obnoxious children, filling the place with entitled guests who treated people like me like shit and responded to silver service with denigration and insults. More often, and worse, were the people I had to work alongside without betraying my displeasure. Dishpigs with glazed eyes who spat abuse in foreign tongues at those of us preparing to satisfy the guests. A chef who resembled a walrus would pour gravy on our feet and smash the plates from our hands if we didn't hold them aloft at the height he preferred. Cruellest of all, though, was the manager I picked for a monster on my first night on the job, the first time I entered her presence. She turned out to be a monster more cutthroat, more merciless, than the one whose reign of terror I'd just fled.

At dusk she called together all the service staff and stood us in crescent formation so she could conduct an appearance inspection. Most of the staff, including me, received a curt nod before she moved on. Then she stopped at one young woman, maybe a year or two older than I was, who wore a light white service shirt over a bra of pale pink. The manager noticed straight away. She pulled the girl from the gathering to put her on display. She stood her in front of the rest of us and made her feel the burn of her own stupidity. She spoke in a voice too calm to suggest real peace of mind, too tense to conceal the rage she kept barely under control. She spoke to the young woman and issued an instruction.

Unbutton your shirt, she said softly, and take it off this instant.

The girl eyed her sceptically but said not a word and made no move to obey.

Unbutton your shirt, the manager said again, and take it off this instant.

A moment's hesitation passed before the girl, uncertain of her motions, gave in and did as commanded. Slowly she unbuttoned her shirt. Slowly she slipped one arm through a sleeve and then, slowly, she slipped out the other. She stood there, still and silent, with her pale torso bared but for the criminal bra that covered her breasts. The manager's next instruction came promptly and even politely, but with an authority that few would dare challenge.

Please *remove* that bra.

The girl said nothing in reply. Clearly she was calculating her options. Clearly her hesitation revealed that to quit and simply walk away wasn't among the options she saw. Since I needed the money no less than she must have, I knew she knew that the manager's tone implied that disobedience would mean immediate dismissal.

She reached around behind her back to unclasp. She pulled the bra away from her skin as she fixed her gaze on an empty spot on the ground.

I do not now remember what her bare breasts looked like. I'd like to believe that's the case because I was quick to look away. Truthfully, though, I can't be sure I looked away at all. I know what I was back then. Twenty-two and still a virgin. Hers were the first bare breasts I'd ever glimpsed. Now that I write those words I remember how she trembled as she grew timid and seemed almost to want to draw her body into itself. I felt the humiliation I knew she had to be feeling as well, and instantly I hated the older woman who would so vilify an underling just to impress upon her the need to visit the changing room and come out wearing only white.

Savage wind snapped at the Saltire that flew beside the castle gate. It picked up spray from a puddle and skipped it across the asphalt. Turning aside, I found the path to Granny's Green and the Grassmarket. What I value about the castle, I realised as I descended the stairs, is how a structure so grand remains profoundly beholden to the feral and the wild. It has been pieced together with awesome efficiency and precision. Its drystone walls encircle a beautiful, ordered complex of civilised activity over the centuries. Medieval quarters and military barracks, churches, dungeons, underground chambers and burial grounds, each one an impression of some ancestral human presence, each one a functioning organ in the corpus of the whole. The emerald lawns between them are mowed and trimmed to perfection. The windows capture the daylight outside and channel it into nooks and hallways otherwise cloaked in murk and must. But beyond and beneath the walls, a quiet chaos rages. The crag is a disaster of planes conjoined at impossible angles. It's less a single mound of dark and jagged rock than a formation of mounds, mound upon mound, clutching precipitously at the sky in a catastrophe of agglomeration. The mounds are covered in reeds and weeds. Clumps of moss and hornwort creep out from every crevice. I love that such an emblem of refined civility can be so besieged by so many fecund forces. I love that this little enclave, built to banish any part of the world that can't be suppressed or sculpted to satisfy human comforts, remains surrounded on all sides and frayed at its outermost limits by everything it attempts to stand against.

I lasted barely three months in there, and on my final night I walked away as pained and exposed as the young woman with the pink bra. Some MSP had hired the place to throw a party for his daughter and a hundred friends. I'd handed in my notice that afternoon and decided to bail before my shift was scheduled to end. I'd give the bar to someone else, I thought, and I'd revel in the prospect of early liberation. But something unexpected happened as I was on my way out. One of my colleagues came up to me and told me that a girl at the party had asked him for my number. I gave him the number and told him to give it to her, but I expected nothing more to come of it. I shook a few hands in farewell and slunk through the castle gates to hurry downhill, a free man, back to where I lived in a hostel near the World's End.

A phone call came through as I opened the door. A delicate accent, maybe Italian. She said she hoped to see me again. She asked if I could return to her. I shared the news among the people with whom I also shared a room. A dozen or so were there to overhear my end of the conversation. They gave voice to the desires I could hear in my heart. They demanded that I rush back uphill to meet the girl who wanted me.

Three in the morning, almost midsummer. A spray of stars sparkled overhead, but the blue had not yet drained out of the farthest reaches of the night sky. At the castle the sentry refused to open the gates without first hearing me grovel. At Mons Meg, far from the crowd, I saw the girl waiting for me. A low stone wall encircled the canon. That's where we'd agreed to meet. I found her leaning against the muzzle, making physical contact with more than five hundred years. She stood there alone in what my memory paints as moonlight. She offered a smile at my approach. I did my best to converse in a way that I hoped would lead her back to my bed. As we spoke together, however, she responded with a sort of tolerant formality, as if she was speaking to me out of courtesy while biding her time for some future event. Soon enough a new arrival revealed what occupied her mind. One of the colleagues I'd just left behind came along with a beer in each hand. A greeting and a toast to my freedom. A swig from one bottle as he passed the other to the girl. I realised then that I'd approached her during a lull in some engagement between them, a lull that had prompted him to go and fetch a couple of drinks. I felt suddenly infuriated, trampled on twice over, once by the colleague muscling in on my romantic territory and once by the girl who'd curtailed her affections when a better catch came along.

Because they were otherwise pleasant to me, I said nothing to them about my unease. Instead I tried to stall, to what end I don't know, by musing aloud on the beauty of midsummer nights in the north. Although the sun dips below the horizon, its light doesn't disappear from the sky. Especially from Castle Crag, with a view of the coast many miles away, sunset doesn't arrive until almost eleven o'clock. The night that follows is indigo, never quite darkening into black, and it brightens again with the promise of dawn as early as four in the morning. I pointed out the pale in the lightening east. The other two also marvelled at it, but with a terseness that strained the conversation. Finally my colleague asked me why I'd returned. What reasons could I possibly have for heading back to a place I'd sought to escape?

I couldn't conceal my hurt. I told them both the truth. I said I'd come back because I'd been called for, because I'd been enticed back by the girl who'd been given my number.

A silence broke open between us. My colleague looked confused and hurt, even a little embarrassed. I watched him think through the situation. I hoped he'd simply turn and walk away with as much good grace as he could feign. I hoped he would leave me alone with the girl, would leave the two of us to ourselves, without trying to cause a scene. But then, as my hopes took flight inside me, the girl spoke up and broke the silence.

Why would I ask you both to come back? she said. She turned to me with unmistakable pity in her eyes. I am sorry for you, she said, but I asked only him to see me.

With one hand she made a gesture not to me.

At this my colleague arched an eyebrow.

When was that? he asked. We didn't—we haven't spoken. I was on the bar when someone said you were waiting for me. I came as soon as I could. I didn't go anywhere else, I didn't see you or take any calls—

Then, without another word, the pieces of the story fell into place. The girl had only ever wanted my colleague to return. She'd probably never even seen my face. I'd simply been told by mistake that I was the one she wanted to see. Really, though, I had no place in her vision of things. When she'd spoken to me on the phone, not knowing

I was who I am, she thought she'd been arranging to meet my colleague. As I'd been making my way back to the castle, he'd learnt that she was awaiting him by Mons Meg. I was only an interloper. I had no role to play in the story they'd stitched between themselves.

My body, my entire being, suddenly grew disproportionate to the expanse of the space I stood in. I felt gigantic, elephantine, and at the same time subatomic. I saw what they saw when they looked at me. An aching and decrepit swine, a slavering thing so desperate to know the touch of an unfamiliar girl that he could be summoned there by a nameless voice an hour before the sun came up just to see if he had a chance to get inside her skirt. I stood there in silence, holding my breath, although I felt like a beast. Worse, I saw, it was up to me now to walk away with all the graces I'd wanted my colleague to show only seconds before. It was up to me to salvage whatever dignity I could still hold onto after their gazes had mangled it.

I think, I said as calmly as I was able, that maybe I may not be wanted here anymore.

For a moment I didn't move. Then I bid them both goodnight and turned around and left. Again I saw myself as they saw me, as they watched me go. A hunched and shuffling figure. A sad, dejected washout, shrunken into the shadows. A cretin retreating from a mortification for which he had only himself to blame.

At Granny's Green exhaustion crushed me under the weight of my pack. Heaviness swelled behind my eyes and stood me still at the Grassmarket. Busywork sprang up along the street. A porter shifted from foot to foot outside the glass doors of a hotel. A newsagent put the day's headlines on display outside his booth. A café attendant swished away the sheet of tin that shielded her shop from the night. When the lights inside blinked on I stepped up to the door. I fumbled again in my pocket for coins to buy a coffee. That was the coffee I took to the window, and as I sat there sipping I saw the pedal taxis setting up. The cyclists dragged their carriages to the edge of King's Stables Road. There they perched on their frames to snag the day's first passengers. When I saw them was when I realised one of them might be Niall. I'd forgotten he quit his job selling clothes shortly before I left. I'd forgotten he'd started to make ends meet by taxiing after that. He was humungous the last time I saw him, easily twice my size, but suddenly I recalled having heard that he'd halved himself in a month of pedalling the hills each day. Would I know him if I happened to see him now? Would he know me if I walked past him on the footpath? Changes had come over me too. My cheeks had grown sallow, my eyes as well. My trunk, always lean, had withered into something spare and scrawny, more bone than flesh. Poison had tainted the blood in my veins. It ate away at everything it touched. It had been free to pulse through me for too long before I knew it was there, and by the time I felt its presence the damage had been done.

Outside in the cold again, coffee cup discarded, a turn towards Marchmont brought me to the Vennel. A few steps up, a remnant of the Flodden Wall appeared and formed an angled juncture with the Telfer. Stone beneath my fingertips. Stark against my skin. The coming of day hadn't lessened the snap of the overnight chill. When intact, the wall had encircled the entire centre of the city. It had been built as a barricade against threats of invasion from the south, but it came to serve inadvertently as an enclosure for outbreaks of plague. In the first instance, the walls kept the disease confined to the city. Two hundred people, all pustules and rashes, had been marshalled into a hole in the earth and left helpless but to howl and shriek, forlorn, as healthy folk above dumped dirt upon their heads. Later on, the council chambers were built atop the pit. Anyone else who was believed to be infected would be boarded up inside their home for thirty days, no exceptions. Those still alive at the end of that time, having subsisted on who knows what, would be deemed healthy after all and released to resume their ruined lives. In one notorious case, when a schoolboy was thought to have infected his fellow pupils and their teacher, all of them were imprisoned inside a classroom for a full six weeks. When the door was opened at last they were found to have died of dehydration. The bodies were burned as always, to be sure no contagion survived, but then the burning raged out of control and caused more agony than it relieved.

Wooden buildings across the street went up in a firestorm. Sparks and embers in the wreckage set the rest of the city alight. The destitute and homeless sought refuge from the flames inside the subterranean vaults branching off the High Street. The vaults were cool, even damp, and padded with stockpiles of flour and grains. The inferno couldn't touch anyone in there, at least that much was certain, and so the people pressed close together and hid. But what they couldn't foresee was the effect of the heat on the stones. As the fire licked the walls, it transformed the vaults into a labyrinth of furnaces. The people inside had no way out. As the heat built up and bombarded them, the flesh of their arms and their legs, and their backs and bellies, weltered, blistered, then burst open, curling over, peeling back, withdrawing from sinew and bone. Their organs turned to liquid. Their skin sloughed off their skeletons. They were literally roasted alive. Not burned, not singed, not charred by flames, but cooked like so much meat. Later still, human skeletons were discovered scattered around the edges of the chambers. Why not in a pile? Why hadn't those people congregated in their final moments? Why hadn't they sought the comfort of embrace, the reassurance of touch? The heat had concentrated, intensified, at the centre of each vault. To escape it for as long as they could, the people had fled to the margins. They'd had to break apart and let each other go.

The stones beneath my fingers bristled with striking cold. I pressed my palm against the surface and I closed my eyes. To stare at the stones was to see what? To see how powerless I was to imagine what they themselves might have seen over time. One long section of the wall I touched ran north across the Grassmarket, then at the Geddes Steps it shot up to Castle Crag. The other section ran east through Heriot's School and into Greyfriars Kirkyard. It cleaved the gated crypts from the headstones, veered off towards the Pleasance, and pivoted there to strike out in the direction of Calton Hill. On its way north the wall traversed the Royal Mile, split the High Street from the Canongate. That's where the fortifications once opened up onto broad, untrammelled wilderness, and that's why that part of the city came to be called the World's End. Right there was where I found a bed, in a hostel room that held sixteen, at the end of the first day I spent on the streets. That night and many more afterwards, I lay down and slept in a breach of space the wall had occupied long ago.

Looking back I can see that I was only a mote of dust. I'd floated through things almost listlessly, absolutely without direction. At the time, though, I thought of myself as the beating heart of where I was. I stood at the centre of a magnificent procession and watched it all revolve around me. I appointed myself its observer, its witness, and therefore its custodian. I detailed as many events as I could whenever I wasn't overwhelmed by the exhaustion of mindless work. I'm sure the others fed me whatever details they wanted preserved because they knew, although they hadn't been told, why I was there and why I chose to remain. I wanted to write. That was all. All I wanted was to write. It's true that the stories they gave me to write were fuel for what I produced. More true is that their stories gave me excuses to act the part of the writer. I see that now; I see it clearly. I was writing all the time. I wrote and I wrote and I wrote without end, compelled to be always writing, compelled by all the statues and the monuments to writers and by the words of writers carved into pavements and etched into walls. Hindsight, however, makes me suspect I was seen as a static person. I was always sitting, after all, to set words upon the page. Back then, though, writing was for me an outlet for movement more than for art. It was action without destination, process without culmination. It was a way of deferring the need to live my own life, by making myself appear to others as if always in forward motion.

The connection I made in touching the wall opened up a communion with the past. Every day, years ago, I'd wake and dress and step outside and cross over where the Flodden Wall used to run. The moments I passed in those places would throw my thoughts down the length of the wall to sites like the one far away where I stood to touch the stones. The touch put me in contact with my old habitations, as if a connection with the remnants of the wall could somehow transmit me to where it no longer stood and let me pause there to peer up through the windows at the faces of the people thronged together inside. Beneath my fingers, at the junction with the Telfer, lay stones that whispered over the ground all the way back to the World's End. In the dialect of the elements they spoke to me of the people with whom I'd once shared a life, bringing those people back to me where I stood on the stairs.

Slices of experience. Slivers of past encounters. Helplessly watching Andrej declare his triumph over me. *Zwischenzug,* chuckle, checkmate. Offering Magda a chocolate bar as thanks for some small favour and watching her fall apart, bawling inconsolably. As a girl growing up in Kraków, I'd learnt, she'd only eaten chocolate when it was rationed to her family and she still wasn't used to seeing it sold for pennies wherever she went. And the others? Too many fragments flew past for me to catch them all and sift through them, and sort out the ways the strands of various stories intertwined.

Lars embodied everything I'd longed to find inside myself. Self-assurance, self-possession, composure and aplomb. Despite his gifts, he'd settled for spending his hours ladling mugs of hot chocolate for ungrateful tourists. For a decade he'd dreamed of teaching history at secondary school in Norway. One day, though, he'd seized up in front of his students, found himself immobilised, couldn't move a muscle, couldn't even speak. That was the end of the dream and the start of something else whose shape he couldn't yet discern.

Tassie Tess, flown in from Hobart, jumped from job to job, from pub to pub each day. She'd walk out of one place on her cigarette break and pick up something new, minimum wage plus tips, only minutes ahead of happy hour. Sharon flew in whenever she ended a month-long shift in Saudi Arabia. She was a hostess serving drinks on the luxury yacht of a sheik who spent his days afloat on the shores of the Persian Gulf. Lindsay arrived from North Dakota and found work in a one-star hotel on the sly. Cash in hand, without a visa, she hung around while her boyfriend, Caleb, returned to Bismarck to oversee their application for residency in Britain.

Alice, meanwhile, settled for the most mind-numbing work she could find, balancing the books for a second-rate employment agency, all the better to distract herself from thoughts of the disaster she was running from. She'd recently lost a beloved sister. An asthma attack, an ambulance stuck in traffic. The night it happened the two of them had arranged to meet for dinner. After a hectic day at work, Alice decided to spend time alone at home and called her sister to cancel their plans. If she hadn't done that, she would have been there beside her and been able to help her through the ordeal. She blamed herself for the result. And then, of course, there was Noah, who came to the place at my urging after we met in a pub. He strode through the door like a man ashine, newly engaged to the fiancée he'd known for only a week, and promptly forgot he'd just committed himself to the love of his life. When he spent his first weeks there flirting with Prue, a giddy masseuse from Vancouver, he stoked the rage of Crazy Christina, who wanted him all to herself. In a fury she left the room, left the city as well, and last I heard she'd found new work on a strawberry farm in Devon.

We weren't on vacation, we weren't libertines, we weren't bohemians or layabouts or skivers. We were just people who'd been induced to lead our lives according to complex rules we'd realised were broken. We sensed they hadn't been broken by us and all we wanted now was the space to fashion a new path free from what had brought us here. We wanted to pause the picture while we caught our breath and gathered our thoughts. We didn't know what to do with our lives, but we knew we didn't want to do what was wanted of us. The places we'd been assigned without choice, goaded into without informed consent, only underwhelmed us and left us wanting. Wanting what, exactly? Not more, not less. Something other, somewhere different. We knew, too, that what we wanted wasn't realistic. Pausing the picture could never be a serious possibility. To pause is to refuse to progress, and progress doesn't abide refusals. Progress doesn't even really abide delays.

Joel made that much clear on a night of particular candour. A pudgy, mumbly, unshaven guitarist from Melbourne, twenty-eight years old, he'd only been able to land a job as a sous chef at a rowdy pub on the corner. Returning in the darkness of the early hours to find me alone at a table in the hallway, he drew up a chair beside me and exhaled his exhaustion. In silence he watched me losing myself in a reverie of writing, pen to paper, words without end, until at last he broke the silence with a question barely given voice.

You going somewhere? he whispered.

I looked up from my pages and rested my pen on the table. I shrugged. It was nearly three in the morning. I told him I felt about ready to drop off.

Joel shook his head and said, That's not what I meant. What I mean is, are you actually going somewhere with what you're doing now?

With a nod he gestured at the writing on the table.

I don't know, I said. Where would I go?

The truth was I had no idea what to do with anything I wrote. More than that, the truth was that I didn't care what happened to it. Scribbling words was still the only thing that mattered to me. Movement, not meaning, was why the words existed.

Joel sighed to himself and leant forward. He steadied an elbow on the table and rested his head on his hand. Then he closed his eyes, almost asleep, and whispered out a warning.

Don't do what I've done, he said.

He spoke to me in a hoarse undertone. He spoke in a drawl, with no feeling in his eyes.

Whatever it is I've done wrong, he said, try not to do the same. Look at me now, look where I live. Every morning I wake up to the sound of bums pissing out booze in the wynd outside the window near my bed. And look at my nights. Look where I have to work. That's where all my energy goes. I thought I was meant to play music. Music was meant to be my life. It *was* my life, when I left home. But now I'm here, and I'm twenty-eight years old, nearly twenty-nine, and I've missed out on the life I thought I'd be able to have. I didn't throw it away or anything. It just sort of went. I mean, look how easy it was. How easy it is to end up with a life in ruins. Do nothing meaningful for long enough and the whole thing just crumbles. It's dust between your fingers. And so now

I have nothing real, no real life, you know, I don't have any *love*—

He stopped there to reconsider what he was trying to say. Then he started again.

I haven't got anything else, he said, to make up for not getting what I wanted.

I didn't say anything to this. At that time my heart went to Çeren, who slept in the bed beside mine, and just as much as I yearned for her I knew that Joel yearned for Kirsty. She was also from Melbourne, a little bit older than he was, and although she worked an even more demeaning job as a waitress at a fleabag hotel, she never let her troubles erase the smile that brightened her face. Joel rose from the table, scraping the legs of his seat over the scuffed wooden floorboards. He'd grown distant from me. I watched him shake his head to himself. Don't do what I've done, he said again. As he turned away from me I heard him mutter something like, I think I blew my chance.

I didn't believe that was true of him. Since I was six years his junior, I certainly didn't believe it could be true of me. Shortly after he spoke to me, though, I started to feel as if I was maybe following his trajectory. At that time I'd made arrangements to sweep the hostel floors and clean the bathrooms each day in exchange for a rent reduction. All I wanted was to write. If I could curtail the cost of living, I supposed, I'd be able to reclaim the hours

I'd otherwise waste on work I didn't want to do. In the meantime, Brett had arrived. He was a redneck Canuck from north of the Arctic circle, a man the size and shape of a bear and almost as hairy as one. He found work as a bouncer at a comedy club in the New Town, and at the end of his Saturday shifts he reliably came home drunk beyond all reckoning. One Sunday morning, just before dawn, he returned so wasted he thought the bathroom was inside the bedroom he shared with more than a dozen others. Çeren woke, in the dark, to the stench of human shit. She found a brown lump the size of a grapefruit in the middle of the floor. She shook me awake to show me where it sat and she asked me, as the cleaner, to get rid of it right away. She told me I had to do it. We couldn't sleep in a room with that thing fouling the air.

I refused to touch it. Anything more than the dirt of daily business wasn't my duty to clean. Çeren and I tried to wake Brett, but we found him almost unconscious. Nevertheless, someone had to deal with the turd. It sat there, sludgy, exuding foetid vapours that seemed to grow thicker and more aggressive as time went on. At last, with gritted teeth, with something curdled rising in my throat, I slipped my hand into a plastic bag and knelt before the monstrosity. It warmed my palm and slopped, spongy, around my fingers. I threw it away and I washed and disinfected the beshitten site and after that, after dawn arrived, I didn't speak a word to Brett. I couldn't.

I went through my day, I did the job I'd agreed to do, but then, with an odour to my person and with Joel's words fresh in my mind, I quit as the cleaner and I couldn't live there after that. Couldn't afford it, couldn't stomach it, couldn't stand the enclosure anymore. I felt myself newly constricted by the unstoppable progress of time. I'd cleaned up the filth as part of a plan to buy myself time to write, but all the time I'd had to spend cleaning stopped me from writing as I'd wanted. I couldn't focus, couldn't concentrate, sometimes I could barely breathe. With every beat of my heart I felt hunted by the ticking, ticking, of relentless life.

Icy wind raced through the Vennel and hastened me on my way. I turned and tucked my chin into the collar of my coat, walked on and exhaled a cape of fumes over my shoulder. The Heriot's edge of the Flodden Wall extends to Quarter Mile. It led me in the direction of the refuge I'd entered to avoid a fate like Joel's. I'd moved there with a hunger for something new to begin. What drove me there, though, was the fact of the hunger, its incessant rumbling, not the misty promise of a place to become who I wanted to be.

A job at the zoo turned up. A chance to work like a grunt, but at least away from the hawkish gaze of my overlord at the castle. A costume would be mine to wear. Enormous fluffy ears. Eyes of twinkling blue. A soft black lump for a nose and a stupid grin. A pantomime koala was supposed to attend children's parties. He was there to dance like a fool and pose for pictures with the birthday boy or girl. I sat for my interview in a suit I'd purchased for the occasion. It cost me every penny of my savings, plus an agreement to pay the balance in instalments for six weeks afterwards. I wanted that job, I wanted it badly, and since nobody else had applied, it was mine for the taking. But what got me the job were the lengths I went to, to make sure it'd be mine. The woman who'd be my boss soon enough walked into the interview room, eyed me in my slick new clothes, and said, almost shocked, You poor, poor dear. The job's all yours if you're keen. You can start whenever you like.

I seized it on the spot and quit my other job when I showed up at the castle that night. No more sycophantic smiles. No more abuse from senior staff. No more kowtowing to the culinary predilections of the crudest members of the upper crust. But I couldn't say there'd be no more shame, no more degradation. I was turned away like a beggar by the Italian girl and her new sweetheart. Their gazes still stung as I slipped into costume for the first time the morning after. That evening and every evening that followed, I stumbled home covered in grime. Perspiration from the ghastly heat of a costume covered in layers of hair. Stale sweat unlocked from the previous day's work in an outfit nobody washed. Even so I earned more money than I'd been making at the castle, and that extra money fed the hunger that had started driving me. I found a bed in a boxroom, really a windowless cupboard, in a horrid little flat a block back from the Meadows. I was happy to find it. At least I wouldn't have to clean any shit besides my own.

Three others haunted the place. I never connected with any of them. Shao flew back to Beijing without warning a month after I moved in. When none of us had seen him for a week or so, we opened his door to check on him and found his room a hovel. New forms of life were sprouting from puddles of congealed Bolognese on a dozen unwashed dinnerplates. Streaks of nicotine stained the walls and mould crawled over the carpet from a pile of wet towels in a corner. Bookshelves overflowed with lad's mags whose pages stuck together. Most of the porn went to Scott, the only native I ever lived with, who claimed it as compensation for being stuck in a bedroom larger than mine. An outspoken dipshit from Perthshire, a brash, belligerent wellspring of complaints, he was so monumentally vacant in any matters demanding intellect that I finally couldn't bear to be near him after a day under the same roof. But he and I were left to ourselves when Miguel pulled a midnight runner and the landlord yanked our lease. Late one night at the end of the year, having woken to go to the bathroom, I found Miguel with a suitcase in hand and one foot already out the door. He was flying home to Madrid, he said, to spend Christmas with his parents. I wished him a safe journey and watched him close the door behind him. When I properly woke in the morning, I found our flat almost empty. All our shared possessions were gone and a trail of pine needles littered the carpet. I followed the trail through the hallway, down the stairwell of our building, and out onto the street. Across the road I found our Christmas tree jammed into the mouth of a skip. Its sad little trunk dangled out like a limp cigarette in a pair of loose lips.

The following night, a week before Christmas, I'd just crawled into bed when rapier eyes and a sternly set jaw strode into my room. A slender man in a sharp suit stood right beside where I'd laid my head. He had a smattering of silver hair and he wore glasses that pinched his nose and creased his face. So you're the one living here, are you? he asked as his eyes roved around without coming to rest on me. Well, this won't do. This won't do at all. You'll have to be out by Christmas Eve. He was the landlord, I learnt, and he promptly handed me an eviction notice because Miguel, the leaseholder, had flown home without ever passing on the rent I'd been paying him in cash.

That rent hadn't been cheap. In fact it had been so high that even in winter I couldn't afford to catch the bus to work. Every morning I'd trudge the hour it took me to reach Corstorphine Hill. From Marchmont to Tollcross, through Dalry to the Haymarket and from there out to the zoo. Then I'd trudge an hour home with my armpits and back soaked in the sweat of the day. Polar winds froze me to the core, sliced right through my clothes. Bad shoes left me slipping over ice on the bridge across the Water of Leith. Daylight robbery on the job only made everything worse. When I put on the koala costume, my clothes and other belongings went into a staff room that should've been kept locked. At closing time one day, I found the door half-open and stepped inside to find my wallet gone. CCTV footage showed a bearded man in a sports jacket sneaking into the room while I milled around the foyer, inside my prison of heat, and offered a hug to any guest who asked for one before leaving. The man slipped my wallet into a breast pocket with all the assurance of an expert who'd stolen more than once before. Then he found his daughter in the gift shop and led her out to be embraced by me. His wife or perhaps his girlfriend stepped back to snap a photo while the man and girl held their arms around the koala. I didn't know it at the time, and I'm sure he didn't either, but when he made contact like that he pressed my own stolen wallet against me. Before I could report the theft to the police, he'd already blown a week's wages on what would become my favourite whisky. Single malt, smoky, matured for sixteen years.

At the Middle Walk through the Meadows, spiralling paths converge. Striking off to Newington and St. Leonard's, to Sciennes and the Grange, to Marchmont and the junction at Tollcross, they conjoin there like spokes at the hub of a wheel. I stood where they met and looked down to consider my options. Had I suffered any pronounced sense of panic in the face of those old misfortunes? Larceny, eviction, outright theft, the spectre of homelessness, and what did it do to my state of mind? I remembered only assuming that my troubles would be resolved. I remembered the distinct conviction that they'd almost resolve themselves. As if by magic or fate, as if I could step back from it all and watch the jigsaw of my life reassemble before my eyes. As if all I had to do, to find my situation stable, was simply wait out the days it would take for the very turning of the world to sweep up the broken pieces and from the accumulation of wreckage build me something new. In a strange way, I guess, that's how things ended up playing out. Lindsay and Noah had recently rented a flat around the corner from the one I'd been ordered to leave. They slept in separate bedrooms, each awaiting the arrival of a partner living abroad, but they had space on their sofa for me to hunker down until the end of winter. Noah's fiancée flew in from Russia to visit him around Valentine's Day. Caleb came over to move in with Lindsay near the middle of March. By then I'd begun hunting for a new place of my own and Lindsay had pulled some strings to find me a better job. She knew

Sandy by acquaintance and he'd told her he needed staff to work at the café at short notice.

Tollcross became my new base and a new room overlooking the Meadows was mine from the start of spring. Holed up once again in the smallest space in the flat, I was sandwiched between strangers. Niall took the room to one side of mine. Arik and Tanja took the other. Hannah took the largest room on the far side of the flat and Celeste claimed the room beside hers. At the centre of the spiralling paths I could see the bright yellow door to the building we used to live in. I don't mean I could see it with my eyes. I mean I could envision it. At the far end of one of the paths, the jawbones of a whale rose up over the pavement to stand as a makeshift gateway to the Bruntsfield Links. The bones obscured my view of the door. I'd have to pass beneath them to find it.

Morning had now awakened the Meadows. A frisbee carved into the air and then wobbled down to the grass. Dogs dashed after branches and balls and yipped as they snapped at each other's tails. Joggers in shorts and singlets skirted a wallow of muddying grass. Squirrels zipped through piles of rotten leaves. Between two trees a man in a greatcoat and skinny jeans pulled a slackline taut. An old Indian woman opened up a coffee cart near an iron gate. She wore full Punjabi regalia and shimmered and jingled with every movement. From behind me a man dressed like Saddam Hussein whizzed past on a vintage bike, and far off at the heart of a field a swish of orange robes performed the qigong movements of the Falun Dafa.

At the jawbones I paused. I stood and looked towards the yellow door. At least I gazed in the direction I knew I'd find it. I paused but I didn't start moving again. With so many people around me I couldn't bring myself to walk. I knew there was a reason for that. I knew, too, that I couldn't stand still. I needed a spur to action, a distraction from my immediate mire, as forceful as any pen I might pick up and put to paper. Eastward alongside the road. Footfall without thought of it. There was an old wall I'd follow whenever I walked to work at Tollcross. The slump of my backpack, sagging my shoulders, led me to slouch over to the stones. For the time I went on working for Stefan after I'd been assaulted, I'd follow that wall back home and scrutinise the passersby to see if I could spot the man the police had failed to track. I never saw him again. I knew I never would. I couldn't say how I felt about that. Now the wall ended at a pillar. From there I could glimpse the entrance to where the café used to be. The building, gutted, refurbished, was mobbed with beauticians painting nails under purple lights. Turning away, turning around, I came to survey the rolling greens of the Bruntsfield Links and I could see in the distance, unobscured, the yellow door.

People hurried along the paths in front of it. Heads down, ducking against the wind, they rushed to work and to bus stops and to someplace they could grab something warm to drink. None of them were close enough for me to make out their faces. At a remove I scanned them intently, a minute, two minutes, five minutes, ten, before I saw myself from outside and realised that what I was doing was odd. I'd come to a pause again and it struck me that this pause and the earlier pause had probably both been prompted by my encounter with Andrej. I didn't actually want to see anyone I had known before. Or I wanted to see them but not to be seen by them. Could I make myself move now that I knew that much about myself? In any event, I moved. What let me move on was knowing, too, that all of the others had also left the city, except for Niall and Hannah. Even so, I found as I walked that I couldn't avoid imagining familiar faces. They flashed across the faces of the strangers I passed, superimposed upon the features of people coming my way and vanishing with a brush of shoulders.

Why wouldn't I want to see anyone? Why not Arik and Tanja, why not Celeste, why not Niall or Hannah? We'd shared some wonderful times. Dinner parties and rooftop dances. Movies watched by the six of us on a sofa built for three, with heads laid down in laps in a comfortable tangle of limbs. As I write I see that the problem wasn't that I didn't want them near me. Reflexive recoil had nothing to do with it. The problem was that I couldn't stomach being seen in public by chance, being compelled to engage in impromptu conversation. Maybe a reunion would be nice. Maybe it'd start with a smile of recognition, maybe it'd kindle a warmth in the heart. Maybe, maybe so, but I knew it'd also involve more than that. It'd demand a disclosure of my reasons for returning. It'd open a line of inquiry into the circumstances I faced. Even if casually worded, even if pursued with all the sympathy in the world, that inquiry would lead me back to places I didn't want to go. The ravages of illness, the collapse of a precarious selfhood. The implosion of a relationship I'd imagined would last forever, the latest in the scattering of ruins that scar the landscape of my life. A series of losses I don't now have the presence of mind to speak about, and a flight, a retreat, to the last place I felt I really knew, the last place in which I too was known. Why would I want to put myself in a position that would drag all those things out of me? I wanted to be seen and known, but not to have to explain myself. I didn't want to talk, that was it, and I didn't want to be talked to. I didn't want my silence or my evident discomfort to spur the speech of someone else, to plunge them back into the past we shared, to force them to dwell on the distaste of our last days together.

My other five flatmates were already familiar. For six months they'd been renting a place with one last room to fill. They worried it'd stay empty. They worried it was too small to let. I didn't share my history, I didn't account for what pushed me towards them, I only told them I wanted to write and needed nothing more than a smooth surface enclosed by four walls. Arik and Tanja seemed unmoved by those words. Niall and Hannah as well. But when I spoke about wanting to write, I saw that I'd captured Celeste's attention. My words ignited a light in her eyes, a flare of interest that yoked us together and grew brighter and more intense in the first months of cohabitation. French by birth, fiery by temperament, and a fierce, impassioned conversationalist, Celeste, I learnt, was drawn to the notion that I was a person with something to say. I didn't know if I was, I'm certain now that I wasn't, but at the time I didn't care. From my first days in that flat, she and I would spend our nights in each other's company. We'd exchange stories and trade anecdotes, we'd air complaints and embark on tirades, we'd debate issues of great urgency and extraordinary intellectual magnitude, and we'd mutually reinforce our commitment to the politics of the liberal left.

Love came very quickly to me. At least what came to me was something I thought of as love. Night after night I spent hours in thrall to Celeste. That was the closest I'd ever been to any one person in my life. It was the closest I'd ever allowed myself to be. I wish I had the words to do justice to what she made me feel.

We shared our thoughts with abandon but always, always, we stopped short of sharing our bodies. We'd share them someday, I hoped, and the longer I spent in proximity to her the more my body bayed for the touch of hers. That's a pathetic thing to admit. I feel pathetic when I see the admission written down like that. But I've shredded my sanity on the pinnacle of this rock, I've circled around it obsessively, over and over again, to look at it from a remove, from a more distant vantage point, and all I can say after all that effort is that there are no words as exact, as precise, to express how I felt in her presence. The feeling came upon me as if a musical note had been struck somewhere inside my sternum, a single note prolonged as on a mourning violin, and its pitch would rise whenever she drew near, and fall whenever she moved away, and always it would be waiting, poised, for its plaint to lure from her some sympathetic response. How did she cast such a spell? Her beauty didn't issue from looks that took my breath away. It issued, instead, from her way of being, her movement through the world, her style of inhabiting herself. Light brown skin, small breasts, lips of pale pink. Long brown hair hung in tresses, sarongs clung tight around her waist and hips. The task of living in one's own body has always been a burden for me, but she took to it with relish, with a vivacity I adored and envied. I had the vague notion that if only I could touch her, if she'd let me touch her, then some of the comfort she felt inside her skin might be transmitted to me. At first, in conversation, I always worried I'd say something stupid to betray my virginal innocence, something that would make her want to run from me. As we went on talking, though, and as we talked more often, I became convinced that my longing to touch her would be honoured if only I could find the words to usher the moment into being.

I remained convinced of that until the day she broke our bond. She broke it with such sudden violence, and with such absurdity, such outlandishness, that she left me flailing not really to restore it but simply to comprehend the damage. My schedule had me due in at the café just before the lunchtime rush. Celeste had taken the day off work and, like me, she'd spent the morning sleeping late. The two of us were alone in the flat but neither of us knew the other was around. I'd just finished up a long, late shower, sometime close to ten o'clock, and as I scrambled for a towel the bathroom door swung open. I'd latched it too loosely to keep it properly closed. When I looked up I found Celeste standing before me and wearing only a robe. She'd thought the bathroom was vacant because she hadn't heard the shower. She'd opened the door for only a moment before she pulled it closed again and shouted a muffled apology from the other side. I shrugged it off straight away. All I would've been to her was an indistinct form in the mist, I thought. Later, though, I realised that nothing had hidden my nakedness. In fact I learnt that the door had been open long enough for

Celeste to see me and to notice, as I stepped out of the shower, that I don't have a foreskin. That's how the madness began. Writing it down in these pages, I see now how surreal it was and, I suppose, how deeply I've been marked by the experience. But I don't think there's any amount of writing that can explain it away. Events conceived in madness don't adhere to logic. If there's any coherence to them, it's of a sort that mimics the slide from a dream into awakening.

Forget about her way of being. Forget about the spell she cast and the call of one body for another. Back in conversation, in wild and frantic debate, Celeste had a tendency to be shamelessly, shockingly anti-Semitic. The Israeli occupation of Gaza and the West Bank raised her hackles. Plus, a French President she horrendously despised was rumoured to have Jewish ancestry. I didn't share these views of hers, I didn't even like them, but I'll admit I'd often let them pass just to continue to be in her presence. Now jump ahead again to the day she saw me in the shower. Close to midnight all the others had taken themselves to bed while Celeste and I sat in the kitchen and talked. She made a pot of tea and offered to pour me a cup, and as she poured she asked me, without meeting my eyes, why I'd never revealed to her, in any of our previous discussions, that I am in fact a Jew.

I thought she was making a joke that I wasn't likely to laugh at. I forced a laugh anyway and asked her what she meant. I listened, bewildered, as she explained what she'd inferred from having seen me without any clothes. I laughed for real this time, trying to think of a diplomatic way to correct her faulty impressions, but I'd barely begun to speak before she shook her head, a blunt refusal, and showed me she wouldn't be moved. She was unconvinced, and unwilling to be persuaded, that in places outside France, in countries outside Europe, other cultures might have customs that aren't just for Jews.

In our conversations after that she took to calling me a Jew anyway. A good Jew, a reasonable Jew, the one Jew whose singular virtues threw the vices of others into relief. Nothing I said could convince her that I was not, am not, have never been even remotely Jewish. Jewish culture is no more a part of my life than the culture of the Sami or the Creole, the Fijians or the Aztecs. I told her this. I insisted on it. I repeated it over and over again. But nothing I did could change her mind. More than that, I'm sure she shared her false impressions with our flatmates. Arik and Tanja, both from Berlin, suddenly started to show me a cloying, conspicuous kindness. I didn't know what to make of it, I still don't know what to make of it, except to wrestle with the suspicion that it would keep me apart from Celeste forever. She'd opened a distance between us, stretched our bond beyond the point of breaking, and left us on opposite sides of a gulf I couldn't possibly broach. Of course this distance only made me want her with even greater desperation. She had seen me as I really am, unadorned and vulnerable, and she'd all but declared she'd never touch me in this lifetime. The knowledge of this made my body howl for hers more fervently than before. Yet whenever I felt the first stirrings of the music inside me, I brushed against the barrier of the alien culture she'd forced me to wear.

Four o'clock in the morning, a few weeks after her jibes had begun, I woke in bed, alone, to the soft sound of a moan on the other side of a wall. Whispers followed, whispered words, loud enough at that quiet hour for me to recognise the voice. None of us had ever seen Celeste show the slightest affection for Niall, but then, the following morning, while the others were making breakfast, the two of them trotted into the kitchen and announced that they were a couple. Celeste might as well have moved into the room next to mine. Niall had often preferred to spend his nights in silence at his computer. Now, in place of tranquillity, my room filled up with the giggles and sighs and ecstasies of lovers in bed. Any comprehension of what attracted Celeste to that beast lay well beyond my range. Just the physicality of it beggared belief and boggled the mind. How could she adore a creature so immense and unwieldy? Sounds of their pleasures seeped into my space, kept me awake at night and haunted me with things I could only imagine. Her delicate hands on the folds of his flesh. Her fingers raking the fluff that speckled the fat of his face. Her grip on the grotesque skin that I knew he must have kept intact, and the way his clumsy, gargantuan mass would have dwarfed her lithe and graceful figure.

Eventually their indulgences became so loud, so audible, so overbearing, that an atmosphere of unutterable rage polluted every corner of the flat. Even cranky old Crookshanks upstairs complained that he could hear them through our ceiling. Arik and Tanja became so irate that they both stopped speaking to everyone but each other, and the situation hit me with so much force that I couldn't spend even the slightest time in the room I worked to pay for. I'd lost the one space in the world I'd dared to think of as my own.

No inclination to return to the flat at the end of work each day. All my spare time, my time to write, took me onto the streets. I'd look for a spare seat on the concourse at Waverley Station or an empty bench beside a path on Calton Hill. Sometimes I'd find a silent retreat in the grass and reeds of Holyrood Park and I'd write until the dimming of the sky made it too dark to see my words. I became increasingly homeless, more and more often at the mercy of the elements. A booth in a pub or a table in a café might've provided a place to stay warm, but where would I find the money to buy the things that would let me stay there long enough to purge myself of what I felt I needed to write? Even cheaper venues like the Waverley food court never lasted. I guess that's why, instead of sitting, I started walking aimlessly, eddying through the streets without destination. I guess that's why, in a sense, the walking began to substitute for writing, keeping me in motion without real forward movement, using my feet to trace lines across the city in the same way I'd used my fingers to scribble symbols onto paper. But then, too, I guess that's why I felt I'd become detached, divorced, from other people. My activity took me everywhere but to a place of my own, kept me aloof from the lives that whirled around me like so many leaves swept up from the ground in the gusts of a gathering tempest.

One evening after midsummer I walked for hours and watched the last gasp of daylight dim into the deep blue of the season. Back at the flat I fell face-first onto my bed. Friday night drinks had emptied the place, given it a stillness that struck me as uncanny. I lay awhile in silence. I think I strayed into sleep. Eventually, though, a light and hesitant knock at my door pulled me back and drew me onto my feet. Turning the handle, half-expecting to find nothing at all on the other side, I let in a shear of light from the hallway and suddenly stood face-to-face with Hannah. She said nothing to me as my eyes met hers. She wore a set of pink pyjamas, a buttoned-down top and ankle-length leggings, and I saw she had been, was still, weeping. It's possible I'd been crying as well. Perhaps she'd heard me and come to offer comfort. She moved too quickly for me to speak and, still without speaking herself, she stepped past me and into my room and she sat on the edge of my bed. With the cuff of a pyjama sleeve, she rubbed the tears from her bloodshot eyes. I closed the door behind her, softly. She didn't ask me to leave it open.

Of all the people who lived in that flat, I'd come to know Hannah the least. Quiet and slender, even athletic, with narrow hips and a fine jawline, with long golden hair and skin of creamy white, she had a habit of ebbing into the negative space of a group. She'd stick to the backgrounds of parties and gatherings, idle and unassuming, and on the rare occasions that she wasn't out of the flat, she wouldn't really show herself to those of us at home. Until she stepped into my room I'd assumed she was often in town with friends, maybe a boyfriend she'd kept secret. Then I realised she'd been hiding herself because, like me, she couldn't stand to be there anymore. As I watched her resting delicately on my bed, I even imagined her walking the streets in the dark as freely as I did, as forlorn as I was, at exactly the same time I set out. Each of us moved along the same paths but revolved around different centripetal points. We echoed and shadowed each other without ever finally coming together to meet. Wordlessly, still, she watched me watch her, and then she extended an arm and offered me an open hand.

I reached out to take her hand in mine. I thought all she wanted was a token consolation, solace for whatever trauma had brought about her tears. Yet with contact, skin to skin, she drew me in towards her. A light touch, a deft touch, her other hand on my waist, and she guided me down onto the bed so that I might lay with her and hold her.

We lay like that for an age. We didn't speak, we didn't move. I would not have dared. I couldn't guess at what she wanted. Finally, though, she took my hand in hers again. This time she held it against her torso. I felt her stomach, taut, swelling with indrawn breath beneath my fingertips, and I felt it fall flat and swell again as her breathing quickened and deepened. Then she slipped my hand under the top of her pyjamas and she pressed skin to skin elsewhere.

We didn't leave the flat for four days after that. We moved into her room, we shook ourselves free of the crushing confines of my walls, and both of us called in sick at work so we could stay together in her bed.

I don't know why, exactly, we finally broke apart. I worry I did something foolish to make her feel like an imbecile. We'd pursued our pleasures beyond the point of aching, and we were ready to enter our fourth night together, when her hands began to explore me again and on instinct I moved to forestall the bloom of ache into pain. Taking one of her hands in mine, I led her into slowing and softening her caress. I forgot I'd never even touched a woman's body until only a few days beforehand. Cutting ourselves off from the world had cut me off from my former self. Hannah, at twenty-nine, had years more experience than I did. I knew this intellectually and, what's more, I could feel it in her touch. But she also had a roughness to her movements and I saw that, without guidance, she wouldn't adjust her touch to me.

I was a moron to act on that fear. The guidance, the very fact of it, the placing of my hand on hers, appeared to her as an insult. A man who was clearly a virgin was instructing a far more capable woman in how best to bring together their bodies. I could only guess at the sting of her humiliation. Afterwards, in darkness, she thanked me for showing her what I felt I needed, thanked me with what I sensed was actually mock sincerity. Then she made a few comments, offhand and in a tone of levity, which weren't as blunt as calling me a Jew but still put me at a distance by making me peculiar. She spoke of worries about her nails, about friction, about leaving me with a second scar. I'd never thought of myself as changed, as having had something taken from me. I'd never felt, as I realised she did, that inscribed upon my body was a mark of irreparable damage.

When we woke in the morning, Hannah said she thought she might need to show her face at work now. We parted ways to tend to the lives we led outside the bed we'd shared. We came together again on occasion in the dire months that followed, but never with the fervour or the intimacy of those early days. Grappling with unnameable needs, I grew closer to her each time we made contact. I felt my heart yield real affections that honoured the pleasures she brought to my body, but I also felt I couldn't speak of them because she didn't feel them too. I felt she felt little for me, increasingly less, a void, an absence, when she held me inside her now. What developed between us then? The inverse of what I shared with Celeste. Celeste had taken my heart in her hand but never took hold of my body. Hannah, having accepted my body, pulled her heart away from mine.

The moment to show her my heart never came. Our household fell apart too soon. On a whim Celeste dropped Niall. She planned to take up work at an orphanage in Senegal. Niall blamed Arik for her departure. He believed that Arik, as leaseholder, had pressured Celeste into leaving as a way of silencing Crookshanks' complaints. Tanja couldn't handle the emerging tension between the two men. She left the flat before anyone else moved out. Arik, bereft, planned on bailing to retreat to Berlin. The day I came home with my face bruised and broken, I found him in the hallway trawling through his belongings. He crouched above an open suitcase overflowing with clothes, a mantling falcon ripping out the entrails of its prey. I asked him how he was holding up, whether it looked like he and Tanja might be able to reconcile. He shook his head to himself and spoke beneath his breath. He muttered something that I took to be his judgment on the state of his life. It painted a picture so bleak that I repeated his words to be sure I'd heard him correctly.

In ruins?

He shook his head again. That wasn't what he'd meant at all. He spoke again, more clearly this time. *Unruhe,* he said. I'm sorry, I don't know how to express it in English. *Unruhe*. I'm not sure how to translate it exactly. It means something like *unable to rest*. But also, he said with a flex of the shoulders, ah, you know, it means more than that as well.

He meant he felt trapped in a vicious circle of restlessness. He meant he couldn't really relax, he was far too troubled and perturbed, but he was also too agitated to commit himself to a clear course of action, and his inability to do that only amplified his anxiety.

I understood his meaning without quite understanding his words. He shifted onto his knees and bent forward as if his meaning burdened him with a weight he couldn't shoulder.

Autumn arrived and I quit the café. I gave up on Stefan's IOUs and turned my back on Sandy. Despite all that, as winter approached, I couldn't find the strength to look for other work. I couldn't look for somewhere else to live, either. Even if I hadn't lacked the resolve for a fresh campaign of house-hunting, new auditions as someone's future flatmate, another round of song and dance, another traipse from room to room in search of somewhere to rest my head, I absolutely lacked the funds and lacked any viable options. I started living off what little I'd saved from pulling coffees. Christmas came and went. I spent it alone in my room. On New Year's Eve, Niall announced plans to move in with friends on Newbattle Terrace. Hannah went out and found a room in a townhouse on Argyle Place. I resolved to throw up my hands and leave town, go slack and submit to the gravitational pull of London, as soon as my money ran out. I couldn't wait for that day to arrive even though I dreaded it.

I hung onto my space for a few more lonely weeks and then, at last, I found my savings almost dry. The day I left town I went to Hannah's new house to say goodbye. She wasn't there. I didn't know where to find her. I wrote her a farewell note and slipped it under the door. I regretted it almost instantly. That polite little scrawl was the work of a coward's hand, a slip of paper that refused to say the things I really wanted to. I turned my back on Hannah's door in disappointment and disgust. I walked into town through the Bruntsfield Links, across the Meadows and down the Mound. Celeste brushed past me without so much as pretending to know my face. All her attention went to the sister who'd flown in for the weekend to help her pack for the trip to Dakar. The blue sky streaked with glaring white as the sun shone down on long, thin stretches of cloud. In spite of the winter chill, that day was as beautiful as any I'd ever seen. In memory it's still more beautiful than any I've seen since then.

Eyes raised to the morning from the pages of my notebook. Written recollections gave way to Bruntsfield bustling with more life than words could capture. Wind-blasts scuttled rubbish over the links. A lone old man with a rusty putter clipped a ball into a hole. Business suits, bound for work, clutched at croissants and coffee. The sweet smell of yeast pumped into the air from the whisky distillery down near Gorgie, and floating in from the city centre came the first bungled blurts of a bagpipe. A couple of months before I left town, I'd spent a night there on that patch of grass. New Year's Eve, the witching hour, whipped about by winds that fled north across the hills. The gale blew and bellowed so loud that it muffled all other sounds. I'd planned to stand there while fireworks burst above Castle Crag. Those plans fell apart when the strength of the wind kept the fireworks unlit and the night sky dark. So I stood alone in the howling on a night lit up like any other. Knowing I'd be leaving soon, knowing most of us would leave, I wondered how painful the parting was likely to be. Celeste and Hannah had arranged to see in the new year together. The thought of the two of them, somewhere secluded, made me long for them both, even if in different ways, but I couldn't then and cannot now account for why they captured me. Maybe what I really wanted wasn't specifically either of them. Maybe I didn't have feelings for either one because of who she was. That's not a pretty admission, but it's probably true. Probably what I wanted was just a body, any body, to share warmth with me at the end of each day. Someone, I guess, to anchor me where I was. Someone to not let go of, and to not be let go by.

When at last the end arrived, it arrived in repetition, in the coils of a recursive terror. I woke in bed with the first light of day sneaking across my face. I retreated to the bathroom to refresh myself, to take a shower. As the door closed behind me, I caught my reflection in the mirror, naked from the waist up, and on the skin on my shoulder blade I noticed a mark, a streak, of pale brown. I froze at the sight of it. Leant in close to the glass. Turned at an awkward angle to better examine the blemish. I probed it with a knuckle, pinched it between thumb and forefinger. I felt a brittleness in it, as if it was less a discolouration than a solid growth embedded in my flesh. Hard and almost crusty to the touch, it sent a surge of repulsion through me. I craned around further, as far as I could, to get a clearer look at it. I flicked it, tapped it, waggled it from side to side. I tried to lift it or peel it away from my skin but it wouldn't move. I forced a fingernail underneath it and tried to lever it off. A spasm of pain, a flinch, but first a glimpse beneath its surface. A clench of the teeth when, to my horror, I saw it binding itself to me with thin white strands or threads, adhesions, textured like a cobweb. Releasing the growth made me realise what it was. It was bark. It was the bark of a tree. It was bark that had grown on me like a scab, pushed up through blood and muscle to settle on my skin with edges ringed by inflammatory red.

Suddenly a sensation of heat seared the length of my arm. My shoulder shattered apart, splintered into countless shards of bark, then combined and cohered again into a solid shell. No time to take it in. Bark raced over my body to encase my every limb. It spread across my forearms and chest, and down the sides of my torso, the way a crashing wave on a beach slides across the sand. I spun round and clutched at my hands in a shock of pain. Blood began to flow down my fingers where twigs had pierced the nails and curled into tiny talons. At my feet I felt the floor shift and I heard a ceramic smash. My toes writhed with serpentine tendrils that twisted into gnarled roots and burrowed down, of their own accord, through broken tiles, in search of soil. Now I returned my gaze to the mirror and saw myself in another form. Outstretched arms of sap and rind and peeling wood. Hair spun into vines that dangled in front of my face. I'd hardly started to scream before bark snapped over my mouth like a muzzle. One last look in the glass revealed my new reflection. Then the bark shuttered my eyes and plunged me into darkness. The silence took a moment to settle in. Disoriented in a coffin of soundless black. Imprisoned in a void whose dimensions I couldn't survey. I felt myself swayed by a breeze that wafted in from somewhere unseen, unseeable. I remember worrying then that anyone who saw me like that wouldn't be able to see me at all. My most urgent concern in that situation was that anyone who looked upon me would be taken in by my flittering surface, by all the leaves quivering faintly in the wind, and that they'd never be able to see the integrity of the whole, the soul inside the structure, the I beneath the way things appeared to the world.

That dream recurred, day after day, every day in the weeks that led up to leaving. The worst of it wasn't the dream itself. The worst of it was that I'd be locked inside for hours at a time, imprisoned in that tree, before my body would wake and permit me to escape.

I'd tumbled into that dream again that night in the wind on the Bruntsfield Links, and I tumbled back into that night when the morning gale awakened the dream. That New Year's Eve, I remembered, I'd wanted a life beyond my reach, and wanting it so badly made me want instead to be blown apart, to be blown away by the wind. I wished the gale would use its awesome strength just to strip me from the world, disintegrate my body an atom at a time, dissolve me into its blusters and scatter my soul across the land. I wished it could unmake me so I might have never been.

I remembered having that want because it, too, returned to me while I sat and penned notes of earlier things. As the breeze baffled the pages of the notebook in my lap, I wished the wind would now strip me away no less than I'd wished it before. Argyle Place was only five minutes east of there on foot. Newbattle Terrace, five minutes southwest. I had no greater task before me than to knock on a door and ask a person I already knew if they might offer me a place to sleep for a while, and yet, no matter which door I chose, the demands of that task kept me shackled to the spot, stopped me from rising and walking where I knew I must, drained me of the strength to speak the necessary words. I didn't make a move for either place. The only movements I made were the ones that captured sentences, affixing ink to paper across the desert of the empty page. Word by word I kept sketching my map of a city that hasn't existed for years.

Day had begun but the sky had started clouding over again. Wind blew strong and with each moment it blew stronger still. Hungry, exhausted, anxious to my bones, I was now fully six years older than Joel had been when he'd whispered his lament to a stranger six years his junior, and somehow I'd arrived at a place where I was without a home, without a grounding, without a sense of my possible selves, starting everything over again for the third time in my life. All I wanted most in the world was to subtract myself from it. I wanted only to withdraw, to become an absent being, and so to sit there and write, to write and continue writing, to be sustained, if not fed and warmed, by everything I'd been able to write and by all the writing yet to come.

Just before I quit the greasy spoon, I had to show a new waitress how to do her job. Friendly but overeager, a year or two older than me, she hid her rakish figure beneath a frumpy woollen cardigan. On day one she admitted that she'd packed up her old life in Bristol and left it all for a new life in the north specifically, *specifically,* to take that shitty job. She said she hadn't been able to find any work in Bristol for months. Now she was happy to have been offered something that would at least keep her off the streets. Two weeks later she took me aside for a talk and completely broke down. She couldn't understand why she hadn't made a single friend in the short time since she'd arrived. She worried it meant she'd failed somehow, or carried within her some flaw that wouldn't allow her to stay. She was gone by lunchtime. I never found out where she went.

What looks like a city is really only barely more than a village. To wander it is to encounter the same array of strangers, over and over again, each one endlessly crossing the paths roamed by all the others. I remember one woman, wide-eyed and elfin, who I saw each day stacking shelves at the store where I'd buy my lunch. I once saw her in the city as the two of us boarded a bus to Portobello. I once saw her in conversation with a friend outside a salon in Stockbridge. I once saw her alone at a film at the Cameo Cinema, and I once saw her, tipsy, leaving one of the nightclubs along the Cowgate. Without any effort I picked up pieces of this stranger's life. She wasn't the only stranger whose life I could partly assemble. Possibly, then, some of the people I passed on the streets could do the same for the stranger I was to them.

Above all, above all, I'm averse to any remark that requires me to explain myself. To be called to account for some anomaly in the normal course of things is more than I can withstand. Every word of it tortures. Has it always been this way? Whenever I foresee a situation in which I might have to justify my presence, I'll try to prepare a response in advance, to rehearse a performance to blunt the shock of sudden exposure. When asked to speak on the spur of the moment, I'll speak and stop and try to speak again, and then I'll circle the drain. I'll spend hours revising and elaborating and qualifying my reactions, all to no end but my own belated comfort. These explanations of myself occupy my thoughts all the time. I suppose that's so because I'm forever looking for ways to evade them.

A retreat from Holyrood Park by way of Croft-an-Righ. Cobbled alleyways in a tangle behind the walls of the abbey ruins. At Abbeyhill the ghost of myself dragged a mugger towards an oncoming car. Back at the edge of the Bruntsfield Links, the rimrocks around Arthur's Seat and the summit had risen over the trees of the Meadows. Promises of solitude, promises of solace. I crossed the grass to cross the Causewayside, close to where a former self felt moved to connect a fist with a face. Further on in the same direction, I came to the Warden's Croft along the crags at St. Leonard's. Enormous black slugs slathered across sodden reeds. Fresh mud gave the morning air an earthy spice, and forced a backsliding tread uphill past the Hawse and Echo Rock.

From Croft-an-Righ to Jacob's Ladder. The slope towards the tower built in honour of Robert Burns slowed me to a mindless plod. Buildings angled along the ridge on the other side of the valley like bones out of joint in a broken spine. Backdropped by cliff faces, earthen tones, slats of chiselled ochre, they looked like rude habitations hewn in haste from muck. Lowlying clouds amassed over Holyrood Park. They swallowed up where I'd wasted most of my day, thickening over the grass and gauzing the air with the buzz of silver sprinkle. I'd slipped over matted reeds and scrambled over wet stones to reach the cairn atop Arthur's Seat. Wet clothes and hair and muddied hands were proof of elemental contact. None of it, though, was proof of an ordeal. While my body had been passing through that filth and saturation, my mind, elsewhere, had vanished my surroundings. They only came into sight again when I turned back to see the place where my attention had started to wander and I watched the mist occlude the scene. A descent at Jacob's Ladder brought me to Tollbooth Wynd. There I turned my thoughts to where they'd wandered while I walked the hills.

Where Queen's Drive skirts the Raven's Rock, over the saddle of Samson's Ribs, I'd fallen backwards into a day from long ago. That route had once taken me into a solitude so pure and absolute that in memory it sparked elation. One of those dun-coloured days like the inside of a rolling marble. The enormity of brilliant blue was mottled by clouds that caught in the sweep of seaborne winds. Whorls of silver and white warped from shape to shape, scourged across the sky towards the hills on the horizon. Days of that sort flicker between the darkness of slate grey obscuring the sun and a vibrancy so astounding, so aggressively blinding, that every aspect of the encompassing world, from the rich marine of roiling lochs to the gold of bending deergrass, from the emerald of moss and liverwort to the ruddy red of flaking stone, has its true colour thrust upon it in vigorous bursts of light and then, when darkness returns, secretes a shaded afterglow. At Woodpecker's Gully I glanced back at how, that day, I'd stepped off the road to stay awhile at Samson's Ribs because something I couldn't name had moved me to linger there. David Hume would've disparaged valuing instinct over intellect, but I am my body as well as my mind and I can't deny what the body wants. I stopped. I vaguely sensed that I stood on the verge of some imminent reward from the world, some gift for being present to bear witness to its wonders, and that this warranted a pause, an idling of time, there where the hillside plunged through patches of briar and thistle and hawthorn to the pebbled brim of Duddingston Loch.

As I knelt to sit on the grass I saw the first swift swoop past. A sleek black slice through the air, a streak against distant hills, it shot around behind me to rouse up the rest of the flock. Speed and grace flew forth as first a few and then a dozen and then two dozen birds took wing to pivot around me where I sat. At times they cut close enough for me to hear the snip of their wings as they swerved to avoid a collision. They staged a riot of perfect orchestration, flakes of charcoal glitter sailing high on skyward gyres, and I marvelled at the privilege of having been there, then, without another spectator, to watch it all unfold for my eyes alone.

Across the Royal Mile, alongside the Canongate Kirk, downhill through Hammerman's Entry to swing towards the Pleasance. I'd moved on to Dunsapie Loch, I realised, with now no memory of leaving behind the swifts to reach the path to the summit. A turn at the shore opened onto the slope between Crow Hill and Arthur's Seat and only there did I remember, at the arch of the fort in the brambles, having followed that path the day I'd seen the summit empty. A couple of corvids skipped over the grass to launch themselves into the wind. Others had already flown and hung high above me, almost static, in battle against the billows. There's a knoll at the edge of the scree that scores the mountainside. I'd paused there and turned around to take in Winny Hill, nearby, to trace with my eyes the dip it makes beneath the flat line of the faraway sea. Still no other person had wandered into view. Only empty footpaths stretched across the slopes. Despite the bombast of the growing gale, I made myself stand fast. I stood and I gazed out in wonder at the drama that unfurled at my feet.

High on a hill overlooking the water came a sense of being submerged beneath waves. Fast winds roared across the Firth of Forth and found the path that steepens at the Laing Rig, twisting around the contours of the dint between my knoll and Winny Hill. Eddying, funnelwise, in that dint, they washed over the bulrushes, bending and bowing the stalks in ripples to wend the grass like seaweed asway in a deepwater current. As the reeds stood up with each breath in and swooned with each rush out to sea, flaxen coruscations shuddered green and back again, and as clouds obscured the sun their shadows fell to earth and lilted, smokelike, in a rise and fall over braes whose swells gave the scene the look of a seabed rippling with colour as light plays upon the surface. But now, of course, I see, having set this down in black and white, that I can't convey the power of what stirred me then. What stirred me was the whole, the totality of sensation, the integrity of every element. Words, clauses, sentences are too relentlessly linear to do justice to something like that. They tease out the threads of the whole and mould them into an accretion of detail observed, remembered, and written about in a way that betrays the simultaneity of the senses. They can't throw together the alchemy of stimulation and solace that made that moment what it was, an alchemy that even now makes every moment what it is.

The Pleasance sheltered the ruins of the Flodden Wall. The Cowgate narrowed the world with buildings clustered beneath bridges that segmented the sky. I'd spent barely a minute at the summit of Arthur's Seat. Being there brought out memories of a longer time spent at the top. I'd seen it earlier, empty of life, radiant with a treacly light before it dimmed to umber when still more clouds obscured the sun. I'd come to the cairn that marks the true height of the hill, atop a boulder worn smooth by centuries of tramping feet. The wind threw all its force against me. An especially aggressive gust nearly tumbled me over the edge. That's why the place was empty. Nobody else who might have come had seen the sense in risking their safety. Nevertheless when I took a step forward to stand right at the precipice, sending tiny stones skipping over the edge, I felt so utterly safe, so assured by where I was in the world, that I might've simply let myself go and fallen forward, off the cliff, with faith that the wind would never let me drop, that it had strength enough to force me upright before I could even leave the ground. To look out then at the surrounding city was to be stilled inside, at last, by a peaceful, placid tethering to a place whose intimacies I knew, even as the wind raged around and over my body and up from the base of the cliffs beneath me. Everything, all the world, from Berwick in the east, across the Firth of Forth to Fife, with Calton Hill to the north and Corstorphine Hill northwest and the Balmoral Hotel beneath them both, from the sterling sheen of Waverley Station to the great black slash of the monument to Walter Scott, from the castle atop its chaotic perch, hunkered down upon the rock that cut deep into the gardens, all the way across the Meadows to the Pentlands in the south and the nearby crags that crabbed the vista before my eyes: everything, every part of the world, had been fixed firmly in place and had a name I knew, a name I could call it by, and it anchored me with a sense of self as one who stood at the core of it all. The city had arranged its pieces laterally about me. The effects of the elements revolved in all directions above and around the space I occupied. The solitude that made this scene wholly mine brought me into a singular moment. It might still be the happiest moment I have ever known.

Then came the clutter of the Cowgate and the curve of Candlemaker Row. The slog uphill along the edge of Greyfriars. Headstones covered in moss, the pieces of the past to which they testified in silence. Faceless men committing themselves to inflexible moral crusades. Outlaws, under cover of darkness, exhuming corpses freshly interred before turning their talents to murder. Desperation makes demands of you. It obliges you to do whatever is necessary to end the pain it inflicts. It sets your scruples askew and either focuses them intently or fucks them up. I can't say what it might have been doing to mine.

The terrier stared into space on its pedestal. Keeping the dog at my back I crossed the bridge that spans the Cowgate and struck out for the heart of town.

If the weather hadn't been so bitter, if I hadn't been so exhausted, I might've followed again the route I'd taken the day the wind drove me down from Arthur's Seat. Along the top of the crags, flirting with their western bluff. Out to the claw of the Cat's Nick, its serrated rocks beneath me. Over Winny Hill and down through the weeds to St. Margaret's Loch. Alone, I might have owned the place, but this time I hurried out, harried by the ravaging cold, and loped down to the Hawse and squelched through the Hunter's Bog. A descent of Haggis Knowe in the rain, a flight to Croft-an-Righ, around the abbey ruins, up to Jacob's Ladder.

I watched the clouds move in to engulf my trail. They pulled from the soil more troubling memories while devouring the site of the only one I'd ever wish to keep.

Hastiness, huntedness, moved me on. A turn towards the Lawnmarket, a wrench around the Castle Crag. An end to the working day. Buses backed up along the terrace. A view of headlights queued at intersections. Car after car pulled out of parking beneath King's Stables Road. Crowds of commuters took to the streets in the gloaming.

Hastiness came from the dread of having truly run out of time, of having acted free of time's constraints until it strengthened its grip at nightfall. The sprinkling rain dried up close to Charlotte Square. Stockbridge froze with savage cold. No sunset to be seen, only heavy clouds with a tint of pastel orange. Staircase at India Street, Water of Leith. The river's silver surface gleamed with tin and foil, crumpled cans of beer, empty packets of crisps. Wet grass at the park at Arboretum Place. I couldn't care. I knelt. Cold seeped into my trousers. Struggling free of my pack, the sweat on my back tapering fumes into the air, I lay on my stomach and let the water soak through to ease the heat beneath all my layers. The notebook near the top of the pack came within easy reach. Damp had turned the pages to pulp. Loamy smell of soaking earth, sponginess of soil. The elements spoke to me, for me, the words to capture Holyrood. Hurriedness overcame me again as I noticed more people, more and more, mostly the suits just finishing work, rushing through the streets and dashing home along the footpaths. Some hours yet remained before the onset of true dark but I knew I needed to make a choice if I didn't want to sleep exposed.

What I really wanted to do was far from what I needed. I wanted to take off my clothes and let the moisture beneath me cleanse me, wash away the grot on my skin. Once, I remembered, I'd spoken to Hannah of an urge I'd felt, long ago, to make love to the earth. How could I explain something as ridiculous as I knew it sounded? It came to me sometime after that day in the wind at Holyrood, sometime well before that night in the wind on the Bruntsfield Links. I'd been standing on a hill somewhere, encircled by rocks and tufts of heather, when I'd been struck by an inexplicable need to dissolve myself into the whole of wherever I was, to melt away and be subsumed by the world so as to become connected to all its constituent elements. I remember expressing this to Hannah, admitting it voluntarily, one night as we lay in bed, after we'd made love and started making intimate confessions. I knew at the time that it sounded as stupid to say those things as it looks when they're written here. I didn't have the vocabulary to voice to what I felt in any other way than to say I wanted to make love to the earth, to place myself inside it, to be taken within it. Hannah, as was her habit, lay beside me quietly and let me try to clarify. She listened with respect, with sympathy, as if she understood what I meant and didn't think me a fool for having felt that urge or for feeling moved to speak about it. I think I may have loved her for that.

When that moment returned to me, I knew that in fact I had no choice to make at all. My only real option, I saw, was Niall. I felt, I feel, I couldn't and I still cannot come face-to-face with a person to whom I'd revealed that part of myself and been so delicately accepted.

I rose from where I lay on the grass and started for the outskirts of the park. Down through Comely Bank, beneath the arches of the Dean Bridge, to Lothian Road and Tollcross, onward to the Meadows. That was where my feet decided not to stop but to head to Holy Corner and from there to Morningside. I veered onto Blackford Hill as the night sky lost the last of its blue. I rounded the rise until I came to the whispering rush of the Braid Burn which, I knew, ran east through Cameron Toll to dump its flow into Duddingston Loch. I followed it where it took me. At the loch, in darkness, I stood a long time by the water looking up at Arthur's Seat in shadow. The things I thought then aren't worth the effort it'd take to record them.

At last I found the old railway path and shuffled on through the dripping tunnel that runs underground to St. Leonard's. From there, I knew, I could follow spur streets back to Waverley Station. By the time I arrived, I guessed, the day's commuters would've disappeared. What was it, exactly, that I'd find there waiting for me? Maybe the ledge off North Bridge, over the rails. Maybe a spare seat on the concourse. Either way I hoped I might be able just to sit and rest, to breathe, to gather my thoughts and pull myself together. Then, perhaps, I might find the strength to think of something I could do without one day looking back on it in shame.

SPLICE

ThisIsSplice.co.uk

www.ingramcontent.com/pod-product-compliance
Lightning Source LLC
Chambersburg PA
CBHW020557310726
48979CB00008B/1248/J

* 9 7 8 1 8 3 8 0 7 8 7 3 7 *